Ties That Bind

Kathleen Suzanne

TANGO 2

Tango 2 is an imprint of
Genesis Press, Inc.
315 Third Avenue North
Columbus, Mississippi 39701

Ties That Bind

ISBN 1-58571-010-5

Set in Centaur

Manufactured in the United States of America

FIRST EDITION

To my hubby
who has always been there for me

Ties That Bind

Prologue

Today Paloma Ortega intended to tell Raul Fernandez she was carrying his child. She had just started her senior year in college and Raul's new construction business was booming. Things couldn't be more perfect.

She stood at the window and gazed out at the brisk but sunny day. The air carried early fall crispness on the ending breath of summer. Though only early September, the trees had already turned to a glorious array of autumn red, rust and gold; gold that reminded her of the ring that Raul would soon slip on her marriage finger.

The bright afternoon sun played on the building across the street, enhancing the golden glow of the sandstone bricks. In spite of the coolness of the day, within her body, warm and secure, grew a little spark of life that she and Raul had created, a life that would bind them together as a family.

She had just returned from visiting her grandparents in northern Michigan. Suitcases were still piled by the bedroom door. She'd been tempted to tell her grandparents she was pregnant, but they were very old-fashioned in their views on sex before marriage. She and Raul would get married, then she would tell them about the baby.

From the corner of her eye, she caught her reflection in the mirror. She stood sideways and smiled, running her hand over her stomach tenderly. She brushed the long, dark hair from her face, her brown eyes sparkling with happiness. How much weight would she gain? Would she still be attractive to Raul when she began to show her pregnancy?

To busy herself and make the time go faster before Raul came home, she would unpack. She'd just hoisted the large pullman onto the bed and unlocked the tiny lock when the doorbell sounded. She dropped the key on the light blue comforter. Raul? Her heart beat rapidly. Had he come home early? But why hadn't he used his key?

She opened the door to find a very pregnant young woman standing there, not Raul. The thinness of the stranger's face was accentuated by hair held tightly by a clasp at the neck.

"Are you Paloma Ortega?" the young woman asked.

"Yes."

"I'm Helena. You don't know me, but I must have a word with you. It's extremely important." She stood with her shoulder purse clutched in her hands, her knuckles white from her nervous grip.

Paloma stood back, fear and shock enshrouding her. Helena! Paul had told her all about his ex. What was she doing here? Had she come to cause trouble? "Come in, won't you?"

The woman moved into the shadowed living room and glanced around.

"Please, have a seat." Paloma gestured toward the long brown, contemporary sofa.

The woman rigidly seated herself, her hands folded tightly together. Paloma sat stiffly on the edge of the matching chair opposite. "How can I help you?"

The woman's expression was tight with strain. "I don't know where to begin. This is all so embarrassing." She lowered her gaze.

"Just tell me why you've come."

"I'm pregnant," the woman blurted out.

That was obvious. "And what does this have to do with me?"

"Plenty, since Raul Fernandez is the father."

Although the blow was mental, Paloma felt as if someone had hit her in the stomach full force. Her hand went to her stomach to protect the tiny life growing there. "Raul?"

The woman nodded. "Raul and I have been together for a long time." Tears glistened in her dark eyes. "We had planned to get married, but we had a terrible fight and then he met you on the rebound." She held up her hand to stay Paloma's burst of questions. "He knows about the baby. He's come to his senses and realizes he really loves me and that silly disagreement we had meant nothing. We're to be married in three days."

"Why didn't he tell me himself?" Paloma gasped. She fought the terrible sick feeling and the bitter bile of denial that rose at the back of her throat.

The woman laughed. "He couldn't face you. Surely you realize that? He knew it would hurt you and would be better coming from me, woman to woman, you know."

Paloma was speechless. What could she say? Oh, by the way, I'm pregnant too? She closed her eyes and drew in a deep reinforcing breath. "So, you want me to let him go?"

The woman seemed to regain confidence; a smile creased her mouth. "I'm afraid he's already gone. I'm sorry. I don't mean to hurt you, but Raul won't be coming back...except to pick up his things, after you're gone of course." She rose.

Paloma watched as the woman moved across the room and out the door. She fell against the back of the chair. Now what? Raul loved someone else. He'd never loved her at all, had only used her on the rebound. *Dios*, what a fool she'd been.

Her mind whirled madly. She had to pack the rest of her things and get out of there, but where? She rose and headed numbly toward the bedroom. Jumbled thoughts about where she might go, where she could stay, raced through her tortured mind.

One thing was for sure. She was alone now. She could not tell her grandparents she was pregnant. She would never bring that kind of disgrace upon the Ortega family name, never bring disappointment to her grandmother's dark, loving eyes.

Chapter One

"Not another penny! Not one red cent!" Raul ground his teeth as he slammed the receiver on his ex-wife.

Gomez Vega cocked his heavy brow and swung around in the office chair, his eyes squinting as if he had been the object of Raul's anger. "Ouch. Sounds nasty."

"You haven't met nasty until you've met Helena. That's why I called you. I have to prove she's unfit to have custody of Rick. He's not safe with her. I know he's twelve, but he needs supervision and from what I've heard, Helena is never there."

"Just what have you heard?"

Raul perched on the edge of his desk. "Rick himself has told me how he fixes his own dinner because Helena is out and that she doesn't get home until late into the night. And several of our former friends have told me the same thing."

He studied his friend who was wearing a rumpled, light tweed suit, looking every bit the absentminded investigator.

Gomez scratched notes in his dog-eared notebook. "If she's leaving the boy alone, I'll find out about it. The courts frown on that."

"It can't be soon enough for me." Raul reached for his checkbook and flipped it open. "How much do you need to start?"

"Five hundred. If it takes longer, then we'll go from there."

"Deal." Raul wrote the check and handed it to Gomez.

"I feel bad about taking your money, but I need this job." Gomez colored deeply. "Got some bills to pay, you know."

"Don't give it a second thought." Raul held up his hand in a sign of understanding. "You have a job to do and you should get paid for it. I don't expect favors just because we're friends."

Gomez shook his head. "I know, but you've done so much to help me in the past."

Raul slammed the checkbook closed. "Do me a good job, that's all I ask. I want to get Rick back as soon as I can. How long do you think this will take?"

"You never know. Sometimes I get the goods right away and then sometimes I have to watch for a while before the subject makes a mistake. But your ex-wife doesn't suspect anything, so I think this will be a fairly easy case." He stuffed the check in his pocket and pulled out his cigarettes, laying them on the desk. "You told me the boy wasn't yours, biologically, I mean. You're positive he isn't yours?"

Raul shrugged his shoulders. "About as sure as I can be without a paternity test. Helena never let a day go by that she didn't taunt me with the fact Rick wasn't my son."

"*Dios*, man, what about paternity tests? Why didn't you have one done? There's a good chance she's lying, you know."

Raul shook his head. "Never thought about it; I was his father in everything but blood."

"Believe me, it's necessary." Gomez reached for his pack of cigarettes. "Do you mind?"

"No, no, go ahead," Raul lied. He'd only quit smoking a little over a month ago and when someone lit up, he felt the urge.

Gomez blew blue-gray smoke toward the ceiling. "The first thing you should have done before the divorce was demand that test, not just for yourself, but for the boy. Did she tell you who the father is?"

Raul shook his head. "No, and I didn't care." His mind wandered. "I took care of that kid like he was my own," Raul continued. "I didn't have to know, you know. I loved that kid, still do. I sweat my guts out to give him everything."

"Well, if you can prove you are Rick's biological father, it would be easier to gain custody of him, especially if you prove Helena unfit."

"I should have had it done when I consulted a lawyer about a divorce when Helena announced she was leaving...without Rick at first."

He paced the floor, feeling for his smokes. Of course they weren't there. He'd quit and he wasn't starting up again in spite of this latest upset with his ex.

"Then why wait until now to set a P.I. on your wife's, rather, your ex-wife's trails. I mean, if you wanted the kid back, why wait so long? What's it been, eight, nine years?"

"Because I had custody of him for a few years. She didn't want him until it hit her that without him she wasn't going to get any more money from me. And you know the courts, they feel the mother should have custody in most cases."

Gomez frowned. "Not necessarily so. Did she tell the judge you weren't the father?"

"No, she was smarter than that. When he asked her, she said she couldn't be sure. She cried and said I was on the road a lot following the jobs and Rick needed a stable home in one place. You know, school, friends and...well, you get the picture. She played her part well." His voice was cold, filled with contempt. "Now I get word from an old friend she's been running around and leaving Rick on his own a lot. He's a good kid, but he's going to get into trouble if someone isn't there to keep him on the right track, someone who really loves him."

Gomez jotted down a few more notes. "Who's this friend of yours?"

"Here, let me write his address down for you." Raul took the PI's little black book and wrote down the information.

"You know, Helena doesn't want that boy. She only wants my money. It wasn't until my construction company took off that she went to court and got full custody of him and child support."

"How old was he then?"

Raul frowned. "I don't know, probably six or seven."

"I thought so. You had him with you a long time."

Raul nodded. "I did. And it was like ripping the heart from my chest when the judge gave him to her."

"I'll bet. But you do have visitation rights."

"Right. I get to see him once in a while. Every other Christmas and summer vacation for two weeks. Big deal. And if I'm in town, I can visit on his birthday."

"Bad business, all around." Gomez put the notebook away and crushed his cigarette in the glass ash tray. He pushed himself from the chair. "I suppose I'd better get crackin'. The sooner I start watching your ex, the sooner we can get the information we need." He pulled a wrinkled trench coat across his broad shoulders.

"Call me when you find out anything."

"Oh, I'll be in touch." Gomez lit another cigarette as he stepped from the trailer. "You can count on that." With a second thought, Gomez stuck his head through the doorway again. "I just had a thought. You're really uptight, bro. Why don't you plan on going home to Grand Rapids with me to celebrate Cinco Demayo with me and my family? What do you say? And before you answer, remember my mom's cooking, no one makes better enchiladas."

Raul frowned. "I'll think about it." But he was sure he wouldn't. He didn't feel festive, but he didn't want to hurt his friend's feelings.

"Hey, Grand Rapids is only a few hours away from Petoskey. Besides, you need a change to get your mind off things."

"I'll think about it." Raul relented.

"See ya later, bro." Gomez was gone.

Raul slumped to the leather office chair and unwrapped a stick of peppermint gum. Not that it took the place of cigarettes, nothing could do that, but it gave him something to do with his hands and mouth.

His life flashed through his mind. What a mess things had become. If Helena hadn't become pregnant, he wouldn't have married her. Would he have married her if Paloma hadn't run away? Damn Helena for all her manipulating.

His gaze fell to the phone book. Petoskey. Paloma...she had been from somewhere up north. Was it Petoskey? He frowned, searching his mind for the name of her hometown. Paloma was the one person who had made the world seem normal. He stared at the phone and wondered whatever happened to her after she disappeared from his life. He flipped open the phone book and looked up the name Ortega. Nothing. Probably wasn't even the town she had been from.

Thoughts of her had haunted him on and off, ever since she'd disappeared from his life. Was she married with a husband and children? The thought shook him even after twelve years. She had been the one woman he'd have given his life for, the one he had wanted to grow old with. Why had she left like that?

The mists of time surrounded him, causing him to remember that day as if it were yesterday, the day he came home to find Paloma and all her belongings gone from the little apartment they shared. There had only been that short note on the table. I've gone away...please don't try to find me, the note read.

Emptiness and anger had settled around him. He couldn't believe it. Without a reasonable explanation she had gone away, and that just wasn't like Paloma.

She'd been in her first year of college. He had just begun his new construction company. They were going to be married and were planning a trip north to tell her grandparents, to get their blessing.

Their love had been deep and passionate; at least he thought it had been. Had it all been a game to her? Had she only been playing with his heart for her own amusement?

"Paloma," he whispered softly as a vision of her flashed before his eyes; with her long mane of chestnut colored hair, liquid, brown eyes and a smile that would brighten the darkest of rooms. She was a constant memory, iced with hurt and disappointment and a dozen questions that probably would never be answered. But a very beautiful memory nonetheless.

How many times had he seen some woman from the back with long hair and thought instantly he had found Paloma. But when she turned around, it was a stranger. Each time, he had tasted bitter disappointment.

A gust of north wind shook the small trailer he'd made into his office on the site overlooking Michigan's Little Traverse Bay. Glancing out the window of his make-shift office, he snapped to attention. There in the trenches of the newly excavated resort site stood a woman who looked remarkably like Paloma. But then, everyone reminded him of her.

He grabbed his jacket, rushed from the trailer, slamming the door behind him. His heavy work boots made a determined crunching sound in the loose gravel brought in for the footings.

He drew in several breaths of chilly spring air to calm his ragged nerves. "What can I do for you?" He towered over the bent form of the small, dark-haired woman in a yellow hardhat, a thick, heavy braid snaking down her back.

The young woman straightened and stared up at Raul. *Dios*, it was Paloma. He couldn't believe his eyes.

After all these years to see her again...She was just as beautiful as when he'd last seen her. Liquid, brown eyes that sparkled in the sun and a turned-up nose he'd kissed a hundred times. And that mouth. A mouth that he'd dreamed of kissing for the past twelve years.

Paloma's face paled beneath her tawny complexion, her expression mirroring his own shock. He took in her astonishment and compressed lips.

"Paloma! What are you doing here?" He fought to keep any sign of emotion from his voice.

She raised an expressive brow. "I might ask you the same thing." She climbed out of the trench, dusted the dirt from her jeans and slipped the leather gloves from her slim hands. "It's been a long time."

He noted a slight quiver to her voice and watched the color seep back into her face as she fought for composure. *Dios*, she was still as beautiful as ever. But her curves had rounded out and matured. Tight jeans hugged her hips and firm bottom. Her full breasts strained against the red flannel shirt, making him hungry for the soft generous mounds hidden beneath.

"Twelve years, one month and three days, to be exact," he murmured.

Paloma raised her shapely brow in questioning surprise, her eyes studying him in return. "I was told White Pine Log Homes was contracting this job. I didn't realize..."

He nodded, a cynical smile touching his mouth. "I own White Pine Log Homes."

She cleared her throat, her nervousness peeking through her reserve, and reached down to take the clipboard from the cement block, her cleavage prominently visible and inviting. "There seems to be a little problem with our agreement," she said in a crisp, business-like tone. "We have most of the undergrade in and you still haven't given us our first draw." She was rapidly regaining her composure.

"You work with the mechanical contractor?" he asked, ignoring her comment, fighting the compulsion to keep his hand from reaching out and touching her. He knew she was unaware how captivating a picture she made. Wispy tendrils framing her small, oval face were teased by the pesky wind, giving her that lusty, wind-blown look.

Her lips twisted into a caustic smile. "I am the mechanical contractor."

"You're kidding, right?"

Paloma placed her hands on her hips. "I don't have time for kidding, Mr. Fernandez. I am Paloma Ortega of Espinoza Plumbing and Heating."

"Espinoza...Ortega? I don't get the connection." Had she married but kept her maiden name for working purposes?

"It's very simple, not that it's any of your business. My grandfather, Carlos Espinoza, had a stroke and I took over the business." She cleared her throat. "Now, back to money. I need the down payment on this job to keep the crew happy. My men don't work if they don't get a paycheck every week."

Raul hated this vulnerable feeling that was snaking around him. Where in hell was his assistant when he needed him? He'd left the payroll up to him. "Wait a minute." He threw up his hands, ignoring the charged atmosphere between them. "Since when did you become a plumber? The last thing I remember, you were studying psychology. But a plumber...?" He shook his head in disbelief.

"Circumstances change." She tapped the clipboard. "Now, can we get back to the money you owe me?"

"This isn't going to work, Paloma. You know that. Too much past history." Damn right it wasn't going to work. All the old yearnings were flooding back. How could he work so closely with her and not want her?

"I don't know about you, but I don't have a problem with this." Her brow raised in amusement. "Anything that passed between us was over a long time ago."

He ignored her comment. "How about I pay you for the work up to now and then get another contractor to finish the job? It would be better for both of us." He turned sharply on his heel and headed for the trailer.

"Hey, wait a minute." Paloma rushed after him. "You can't do that. I have a signed contract."

"Contracts can be broken," he threw over his shoulder, striding away without looking at her. He couldn't have her on the job. He couldn't do that to her...*Dios!* Who was he kidding? He couldn't do that to himself.

He knew his long strides were making it difficult for her to keep up, but determined footsteps racing after him told him he was in for a fight. If he suddenly turned around, he suspected he would come face to face with stone-cold fury, a fury he'd tasted more than once in his life.

"I started this job and I'm going to finish it. I have an airtight contract, signed, sealed and delivered!"

"And I have a signed contract with Espinoza Plumbing and Heating, not Paloma Ortega," he shot over his shoulder, knowing his reasoning was full of holes.

"I already told you, I am Espinoza Plumbing and Heating. If you want trouble, I can give you enough trouble to hold up this job for a very long time," she threatened.

He abruptly stopped in mid-stride and whirled toward her. She flew into him with such force he had no alternative but to reach out to keep her from falling. For an instant, time slipped away. He was back in Kalamazoo with Paloma in his arms. It seemed the most natural thing in the world.

His arms tightened like a vice around her slim, soft body. Drawn to her like a magnet, he wanted to taste her lips, to feel her response beneath his.

No. He had to hang on to reality. He couldn't let his hormones rage unchecked like a lovesick teenager. Unwillingly, he put her from him. It was like cutting off an arm or leg to let her go.

Visions of a crackling fire in the fieldstone fireplace and their naked bodies twined together on the bearskin rug surfaced to taunt him. No matter how many times he'd reminded himself she was the past, that she had walked out on him, the mists of time had brought up her image, gloriously tempting and willing.

"This is no good for either of us." His hoarse, raspy voice was low, edged with pain. Undeniable fires of passion burned in his loins. "Let me cut you a check for what you've already done. I'll get another contractor. That will free both of us."

"*Dios! Anda ya!* she laced her anger in Spanish. "*Que' broma es'esa?*"

"Whoa. Hold on there." Raul held up his hands in a sign of compromise. "You know I don't joke about serious matters. We must resolve this and getting another contractor will do that."

"In a pig's eye, it will." A warning cloud settled across her features.

She wasn't about to back down. The determined set of her jaw and the ready-to-fight stance he knew so well told him that. "Okay, okay." He held up his hands in defeat. "I'll honor the contract, but you damned well better do the job a man would do." He felt like a snake treating her so harshly. But he couldn't take the chance of getting involved again. He groaned inwardly. Hell, he wasn't going to get involved. She'd dumped him like yesterday's garbage. He wouldn't allow that to happen again.

His gaze fell to her finger. She wasn't wearing a wedding ring. Not even an engagement ring. *Madre Santo.* What did that mean? Was she married or not? Engaged? What was wrong with him? Why should it matter? There was no going back. She'd made that clear twelve years ago when she walked out.

"I'll do better than any man you could bring in." She shook her slender finger in his face. "I have ten men working for me. Ten damned good men and they do one hell of a job."

"Is anything wrong?" A tall, serious-faced man walked toward them.

"Carl, this is the general contractor, Raul Fernandez. Mr. Fernandez, this is Carl Walters. We were just discussing finances, and in fact, he's agreed to cut me a check so I can pay the men." Her whole demeanor changed from hostile to pleasant in one split second, yet just behind those veiled eyes stood a challenge, daring him to contradict her.

"Pleased to meet you." Carl reached out his hand to Raul.

"Same here." Raul took his hand.

"Carl is not only my foreman but my fiancé."

The atmosphere was suddenly as thick as plumber's goop. Another gut-punch. Of course he'd thought she might have a husband and children. But those were only thoughts. This man standing in front of him was flesh and blood, not a figment of his imagination.

Raul shuddered when he thought of Paloma in this man's arms, making love and giving it. From the cobwebs of the past, jealously reared its ugly head. He knew where she liked to be touched and how. He'd like to think only he could bring out that special passion that set her on fire.

From the day she left, he'd thrown himself into his work trying to forget her. But he'd failed miserably. Not a day had gone by he hadn't thought about her or remembered the feel and taste of her. Suddenly, Paloma's voice pulled him from his thoughts.

"Carl, that Huntley job needs to be measured. Why don't you take the van and get the measurements so I can draw up the job? You know, make sure the blueprints are right. I don't want any more surprises with backward prints." Paloma cooly ordered him away. "I'll meet you for lunch, usual place."

"Gotcha." Carl sauntered toward the parked vehicle.

Puzzled, Raul watched him leave. If this was a real love match, where were the sparks, the passion that lovers wore on themselves? He couldn't put his finger on it, but something was lacking between these two. Carl hadn't even kissed her goodbye when he left.

Raul put the puzzling questions away and threw his jacket over his shoulder. "Come into the office. I'll cut you a check for the first draw."

Paloma followed him into the small travel trailer with a large office desk taking up one whole end. The delicious aroma of freshly brewed coffee filled the small area.

"Have a seat." He gestured to the chair recently vacated by Gomez. "Coffee?" He held up the pot.

"Yes, please." She sat on the black leather chair opposite his. "It's cold out there." She rubbed her hands together. "There's even a bit of snow in the air."

He poured two cups of steaming coffee and handed her one. He knew she was making small talk, trying to ease the tense situation. "Do you still take it with cream and sugar?" he asked, ignoring her conversation about the weather.

"No. Black is fine." She wrapped her long, tapered fingers around the hot cup.

"Seems that's changed too. You used to like it sweet with lots of cream."

"Lots of things change." Her voice wavered uneasily.

"Snow?" Her words finally sunk through his muddled thoughts. He glanced out the window at the small specks of white that had invaded the April day. "Damn, I was going to golf after work."

Paloma followed his glance out the window. "It's not much, just enough to let us know ol' man winter doesn't want to give in to spring yet. It shouldn't hinder your game too much. A lot of guys play in the cold."

"Tell me," he said, turning the conversation back to business, "when will the undergrade be finished?"

Paloma sipped the hot coffee. "It's almost finished now. The men will lay the west section this afternoon and the cement can be poured tomorrow. Everything will be stubbed through the floor and ready tomorrow afternoon."

"Good." No, it wasn't good, he mentally corrected. This wasn't good at all. Tomorrow was three days ahead of schedule. The contract said they'd be done on Friday. Tomorrow was only Tuesday. Damn, this wasn't going right. If she was late, or wasn't doing a good job, he could break the contract, but he'd seen her work. Much as he hated to admit it, her work was neater than a lot of jobs he'd been on.

"Look, Raul. I know this is hard on both of us. This is a large job. There's no reason we have to be near each other. I'll be in and out. You don't have to see me unless you need to."

"Yeah, right." He lowered himself into the chair behind his desk. "Why does this job mean so much to you? I mean, hell, there are lots of jobs out there. Why is this one so special?"

"For the simple reason my grandfather worked on this one before his stroke. It meant a lot to him to work on this resort, and I mean to see he gets the satisfaction of seeing our part completed...by me."

Raul studied her. He heard her words, and more than concern for her grandfather was behind her reasoning. What was really bothering her?

"Look Raul, we're adults now. We can do our jobs objectively and stay out of each other's way. I'm not about to give up this job. Not for you or anyone."

There was no doubt about that. When she got her teeth into something, she hung on. But that was something he always admired, her spunk and spitfire wit.

Her voice broke in on his thoughts. "Not to change the subject, but do you mind if I use your phone to call my grandfather? I always check on him since his stroke."

"No, no, go ahead." He gestured to the phone.

Paloma dialed the number and talked in low tones to her grandfather. "I don't think that would be a good idea...I really don't."

She kept her expression deceptively composed. "No, he's a busy man. I have everything under control."

Raul frowned. He knew her grandfather had asked to speak to him. He pulled the phone away from her ear and placed it to his own. The warmth of the earpiece, warmed by her body, mingled with the intoxicating scent of the light fragrance she wore. Collecting himself, he said, "Raul Fernandez here."

Paloma sat back, her arms folded belligerently across her chest. Averting his eyes from her angry expression, he concentrated on the voice at the other end of the line. "Dinner? At your house?" He was too startled to offer any objection to the unexpected offer.

Paloma slumped back in her chair, her expression reflecting her own misgivings.

"Thank you for the offer, sir, but I did plan on paperwork this evening."

Raul nodded as he listened. "All right. I suppose I can do that. I'll see you at seven." He replaced the receiver.

Paloma rose, picked up her hardhat and stepped toward the door.

"Aren't you forgetting something?" Raul's voice stopped her.

"What?" She turned toward him.

"Your check." He handed her the piece of blue paper that sealed their deal.

"By the way, where does your grandfather live?"

"Live?" Surprise crossed Paloma's face.

"His address. I have to know if I'm to meet him for dinner."

Paloma flushed under his scrutiny. "Yes, of course." She reached for the pen beside the scratch pad and scribbled down the address. When she shoved the paper and pen toward him, their hands touched. For a brief moment, he knew she felt the sparks that flew when their skin connected. Quickly she pulled her hand away, denying him the opportunity to touch her again.

Their gazes locked and for a few pregnant seconds he was back in Kalamazoo, to happier times when they loved each other and shared a relationship. Her dark, smoldering eyes told him that she felt something too. But he wondered if hate and loathing burned there instead of passion.

Straightening herself, she shoved the check in her shirt pocket. "Thanks," she said, her expression blank. "I'll do my best to stay out of your way." The words came out edged with bitterness.

For a brief moment their gazes locked and held. Then she spun on her heel and rushed through the trailer door, leaving him unsettled and troubled with their encounter.

❦

"Pop, I can't be here for dinner. I have to be with Carl on the Huntley job."

"Not tonight, *nina*. Tonight is very important."

Paloma didn't want to argue with her grandfather. But seeing Raul again had been too upsetting, had brought back memories she had thought deeply buried. Dinner with him would be more than she could take at the moment.

If she didn't need this job so badly to take the company back in the black, she'd tell Raul to shove it. But they were strapped and this job meant pulling them out of the red. She couldn't tell her grandfather that either. He would just worry if he knew they had lost money this last quarter.

"Listen, *nina*. If you're going to be Espinoza Plumbing and Heating, you're going to have to do it all. Wining and dining the general contractor is part of that job."

"Carl needs me more." She twined the hairs from her braid around her finger nervously.

"Do you want to stop hedging and tell me what's really eating you?" her grandfather asked. "And don't give me that bull about Carl needing you."

She threw the braid over her shoulder and bit her lower lip. "I don't know what you mean..." Her voice trailed off when her grandfather cocked his head and frowned at her.

"Le di diez pesos por esto!" He reverted to Spanish as he sometimes did when he was upset and rolled his eyes in exasperation. "Something's bothering you. Bothering you bad. Is it this Raul Fernandez fella? Has he done something he shouldn't?"

Could things get any worse? She'd rarely been able to keep things from him, but the baby was something she'd had to keep secret. Paloma met her grandfather's gaze steadily. "Good heavens, no. Where did you come up with an idea like that?"

"From you. I've only seen you this jumpy once before, and that's when you came home from college that fall you changed colleges. I couldn't get the truth out of you then either."

Paloma stood motionless in the middle of the room. All the old anger and hurtful wounds she'd worked all these years so hard to suppress opened afresh, raw and painful. All control over her emotions snapped.

"Pop, I..." For one split second she was about to unburden herself. But she swiftly gained control.

An embarrassed flush stained her face. "Okay, I have problems. But they're my problems and I have to solve them." Guilt flooded her. Nevertheless, he must never know about the baby or Raul. That was all in the past where she intended to keep it.

"Let me help you, *nina*."

"Not this time."

"What's an *abuelo* for if not to help his little *nina* when she needs it most?" His voice softened. "Tell me what's wrong?"

Images of Raul and the baby weakened her resolve. And again, for one split second she was tempted to throw herself into the safety of his arms and unload everything. Just as quickly, strength and determination asserted themselves and she lied smoothly, "I'm just tired. This is a big job and I get the impression Raul Fernandez dislikes women on any of the crews. I don't think he thinks I can handle the responsibility."

"Is that all?" Her grandfather echoed the relief that flashed through his eyes. "I can set that young hombre straight in a hurry."

"No! I don't want you interceding for me. I have to handle things myself. Please."

His face split into a grin. "If that's the way you want it. But you tell me if things get more than you can handle. I don't want you keeping secrets from me. I worry more when I don't know what's going on."

He wasn't the only one to feel relief. She wouldn't be able to live with herself if she spilled her past and both her grandparents found out her disgraceful secret. Her grandfather could even suffer another stroke if she shocked him with that kind of news. No, it was best to leave the past in the past. She would get through this thing with Raul. In time he would go on to another job and she'd never see him again.

She bent and kissed his weathered cheek affectionately. "I'll confide in you when I need to, I promise."

"Good. I don't like to think of you carrying a burden and not letting me help."

She had to be much more careful from now on. Her grandfather couldn't afford to fret about her. Her gaze was drawn to the phone. She closed her eyes, indecision surrounding her. "Okay, I'll call Carl and tell him I can't make it tonight, since you feel I should be here."

"Good. I need you here," her grandfather said.

After a short conversation explaining things to Carl, she made her way up the oak staircase to the second floor.

Paloma stood at her bedroom window staring at the gray April evening. Why now? Why after all these years had fate stepped in, bringing Raul back to turn her life upside down.

She never stopped thinking of her daughter. Her birthday, February 11, was the hardest day of the year to get through. Visions of dark, curly tufts of fine hair, a tiny round face and a rosebud mouth played before her eyes.

Guilt consumed her. She'd never told Carl about Raul, nor of the child they conceived together. In fact, she'd never told anyone about the baby. This had been one secret she alone knew; a secret she carried within her heart.

Seeing Raul had brought back all the old longings to find her daughter. Oh, not to try to get her back, or to even let her know she was her mother. She would never do that. But to be content she had to find out if she had a good home and was happy. All she knew was that the family that adopted her was Spanish and Catholic, just as she had requested.

She quickly crossed herself and threw an apologetic glance at the statue of the Virgin Mary on her shelf. It was unthinkable that she had given that baby away, but for a gringo, Protestant family to have adopted her was even more unthinkable, at least in her grandparents' line of thinking.

She hung her head and closed her eyes tight trying to stop the tears. Not only had she kept her guilty secret from her family, but she had never even confessed to a priest what had happened. Was she damned forever? Maybe she should go talk to a priest. Perhaps he could help her sort out her feelings, help her make penance.

What to wear...? She forced her mind off the baby, off her problems. She ran her hands over the line of dresses in her closet. Not the dark blue, it was too drab, the dress she wore to her aunt's funeral in Mexico last year. Not the black, it gave signals of outright seduction with its plunging neckline.

No. She wasn't going to put on any pretense of dressing because Raul was coming to dinner. She would wear casual slacks and a sweater to show him he meant nothing to her now.

She laid out a clean pair of jeans and a green sweatshirt. Removing the towel from her wet hair, she blew it dry and ran a brush through it until it hung down her back in cascading waves, clasping it tightly to her neck with a pearl clasp. Not much makeup either.

Raul was the magnetic type of man when once met was not easily forgotten. Things were worse in her case. Not only had she met him, but she knew him intimately. He had been branded into her soul like solder on copper pipe.

His eyes, a compelling shade of brown-black with just a few flakes of gold, and his face, bronzed by the wind and sun, gave him that hardy outdoorsy appearance. His heavy mane of straight, black hair fell just below his collar. Strongly built, he had a confident set to his broad shoulders.

In spite of his rugged appearance, he seemed sad. She wondered what had happened in his life to make him so. Did it have something to do with his wife? For the first time she allowed herself to remember the woman who had come to their apartment so long ago; the woman who had been his true love.

Chapter Two

When the door bell rang, Paloma glanced at the clock. Seven on the dot, punctual as ever. She had to say that for him. Her heart was beating faster than usual. She felt giddy and apprehensive at the same time. Surely she didn't look forward to seeing him again. What they had shared was in the past. Any feelings she had for Raul were dead and buried, or were they? With one last glance in the mirror, she raced out of the room and down the stairs.

Hesitantly, Paloma paused to take several reassuring breaths before she opened the door. Swallowing her nervousness, she pulled open the heavy oak door with frosted glass panels. Raul stood tall and handsome, with a bottle in hand. Her throat tightened as their gazes met and the years seemed to melt away.

"Paloma?" His eyes moved down her body in an intimate, appreciative caress. "What are you doing here?"

"I live here."

"But I thought...I mean, you're engaged."

A crooked half-smile creased her mouth. Of course, she knew exactly what he thought. She was engaged, so she must be living with her fiancé. "I learned my lesson the first time." Once the words were out, she wished she could pull them back.

His expression was one of pained tolerance.

She ignored the fact he still held the ability to stir her blood and said, "Did you have trouble finding the house?" Her gaze trailed over him, taking in his white Henley shirt opened at the neck, exposing a hint of muscled chest sprinkled with familiar black curls. At the bottom of the denim sports jacket, her eyes fell to his stone washed jeans that hugged his well- muscled thighs.

"No trouble," he said, his eyes twinkling mischievously. His voice mocked her intense scrutiny. "I thought your grandfather might like this." Wearing his composure like a second skin, he held out a bottle of tequila.

"Thank you." For the second time in one day their flesh touched and fire burned. Hadn't she learned her lesson the first time around? Raul Fernandez was a dangerous man. He could turn her emotions upside down, and she had no power to stop him. Then when he tired of her, he would leave her without a backward glance. No, he wouldn't have the chance to break her heart again.

"Aren't you going to invite me in?"

Paloma felt heat rise in her face. "Oh, I'm sorry. Please, come in." She stepped back as he brushed passed her, again igniting the fires of longing. Damn him! Damn his effect on her!

Raul surveyed the Victorian foyer with an appreciative eye. "Will he be joining us?"

"Grandfather? Yes, he's in the living room watching the news. Come and meet him." She closed the door against the cool April evening.

"No. I meant your fiancé," he said with a mocking glint in his eyes.

What kind of game was he playing now? she wondered. Forcing her emotions in check, she answered, "I don't know if Carl will be here or not. He's on a job, one I was supposed to help him with," she said dryly. "Grandfather felt I should be here instead." With that, she turned and led the way across the highly polished hardwood floor and into an old-fashioned but elegantly decorated living room, tastefully decorated with Spanish accents.

There was Mexican pottery on the hearth, and a rug woven in bright colors before it. Several pictures on the wall depicted Mexican life and over the fireplace a large picture of a bull-fighter dominated the room.

"Pop, this is Mr. Fernandez, the general contractor for the Timberland Resort."

"Raul. Please, call me Raul." Raul held out his hand to Paloma's grandfather.

"Everyone calls me Mex. He shook Raul's hand. "Short for Mexico, you know, my nickname from my migrant working days. It stuck, I'm afraid. Paloma has told me about you. Have a seat." He motioned with a less than steady hand toward the red leather reading chair beside the fireplace, where fire licked birch logs.

Raul jerked a steady look at Paloma, a silent question hanging between them.

Ignoring the look, Paloma handed her grandfather the trquilla. "Our guest brought this for you." She held the bottle so her grandfather could see the worm at the bottom.

"A man after my own," Mex said, in his gruff, gravelly voice that usually put people off until they got to know what a wonderful, caring person he was.

"Remember what the doctor said. You can have a little, but he'd prefer you didn't have any." Paloma bent and placed a loving kiss on the top of his balding head before she moved toward the kitchen, from which came the wonderful, spicy aroma of Spanish cooking.

"Nice looking hombre, that one. A little competition for Carl maybe?" Her grandmother winked teasingly at Paloma who reached for the glasses. It was no secret her grandmother had never cared for Carl and didn't mind letting her know.

"I know you don't approve of Carl, but please, don't start on him tonight. And as for Raul Fernandez, he's only a business acquaintance," Paloma returned, trying to keep the irritation from her voice. "I'm sorry Pop invited him to dinner. He isn't quite ready to let go of the business, you know, but he shouldn't be talking business either."

"I know." Her grandmother nodded. "This whole thing has been very hard on Mex. He is not one to give in, even to sickness."

Paloma's gaze drifted toward the hall door. "I worry about him. He must take it easy. But he refuses to do what the doctor says."

Her grandmother carefully removed the tamales from the oven and began arranging them on the platter, dripping a delicious smelling sauce over them. "I've been trying to get him to go away for a while, you know. I've suggested going to Mexico to visit his family, but he refuses to go until this job is finished. So, I thought maybe we could get him to go to the cottage up across the Straits or something. What do you think?"

"That would be great! But can we get him to go? That's the operative word?"

"Maybe," her grandmother said thoughtfully. "It's only a few hours away. And he could get the rest he needs."

"In the next day or so, we'll figure some way," Paloma said, picking up a small piece of cornmeal left in the pan and popping it into her mouth. "Mmm, no better cook in the north, than you." Her grandmother colored. "*Seguro!* You're just buttering me up for more tamales, *nina.* But you'll just have to wait until dinner."

"Okay, okay. Is there anything I can help you with?"

"No. You go see to your grandfather. I will finish here." Paloma rinsed her hands and moved toward the living room that echoed laughing voices. By the sound of things, Raul and her grandfather were getting along quite well. But then, what had she expected? Raul was a dynamic personality who could have the *diablo* himself eating out of his hand without half trying.

"What's so funny?" She forced a smile and sat beside her grandfather's wheelchair.

"Raul watched that same hockey game I did between the Red Wings and the Black Hawks. *Si*, that was some game!"

Paloma rose from the arm of the sofa and slumped down on the overstuffed cushions, groaning. "Not hockey again. Give me baseball any day."

"It's coming up soon enough," her grandfather teased.

"You don't like hockey?" Raul asked, his gaze turning to her.

"No. But I do like figure skating," she answered. A shadow of annoyance crossed her face. She hadn't liked hockey when they were together and she liked it even less now.

"Don't let her kid you." Her grandfather winked at her tenderly. "She loves sports. I couldn't keep her in her seat when we went to the Silver Dome last fall to watch the Lions play."

"Really?" Raul threw her a mischievous grin.

"Why is that so strange?" she asked, feeling frustrated that she had to explain anything to him, much less things he already knew.

"Most women I know hate sports."

"Maybe you know the wrong women!" she answered smartly. "My friends like sports and can talk plays and scores with any man. I just don't happen to like hockey. But I like basketball."

"Detroit Pistons, right?" Raul said, throwing her a devilish grin that almost melted the ice around her heart.

"Of course, who else?" He seemed to love baiting her, making innuendoes to the past they'd shared. Well, she could play games as well as he could. But before she could give her come-back, her grandfather spoke up.

"This girl really does know her sports." Mex patted her arm affectionately.

"I should, *abuelo*, you run ESPN twenty four hours a day." She rose and leaned lovingly over her grandfather, twining her arms around him. "I wouldn't be a bit surprised if he wanted me to buy five more TV sets and arrange them in a semi-circle so he could have all the games playing at once."

"*Si*. That's what I call a good idea," her grandfather readily agreed.

Paloma's grandmother entered the room wiping her hands on her apron, smiling affectionately at Paloma and her grandfather. "Dinner's ready."

Mex waved her into the room. "Inez, come meet our guest, Raul Fernandez."

Inez held out her hand. "I am pleased to meet you Mr. Fernandez."

Raul rose and held out his hand. "Raul. Call me Raul."

"Raul." Inez colored at the familiarity and retreated to her kitchen.

Raul followed Paloma and her grandfather toward the dining room.

"Sit to grandfather's right." She motioned for Raul to sit as far from her as possible. Then her gaze was drawn to the empty place beside hers that would have been Carl's, had he been here. True, he said he couldn't promise her anything, but he could have done this for her because she asked. But he was a workaholic, work always came first with him. But she needed his support tonight of all nights.

"Aren't you eating with us?" Mex looked around for Inez' place at the table.

Inez shook her head as she placed another home made creation on the table. "I'll eat in the kitchen. You carry on with your business meeting and I'll tend to the cleaning up."

Paloma was proud of their home and her grandparents. Her grandmother had been raised in a strict, old-fashioned family. The women ate in the kitchen while the men ate separately. Inez reverted to this way of life when people came for business, especially men.

The large dining room was what one would expect from a large turn-of-the-century Victorian with its high ceilings, and walls papered in soft blue flowers. The oval, oak dining room table was one that had been in Paloma's family for as long as she or her grandfather could remember. It had been re-finished to match the antique china hutch that stood in one corner displaying family treasures and memorabilia from Mexico.

"You have a nice place here." Raul took his place across from Paloma.

"We like it." Mex drew his wheel chair to the head of the table. "But as for the redecorating, all the credit goes to my wife and Paloma. They conspired together to make the house a mix of our Spanish heritage and Victorian architecture."

"Really." Raul arched a dark brow at Paloma. "You seem to be a woman of many talents."

"Thank you," she replied, a tinge of sarcasm edging her voice. Raul obviously noticed since he slightly raised his eyebrows. Paloma ignored his look. "Please." She threw her grandfather an uncomfortable glance. "You're embarrassing me."

"Paloma cooks too," Mex continued, radiating pride in his granddaughter. "We'll invite you to dinner sometime when she does the cooking."

Raul glanced her way, a mischievous smile spreading across his lips. "I would appreciate being invited to a meal prepared by your capable hands." His mocking gaze held hers.

"Then we'll make it soon, won't we, Paloma?"

Paloma pulled her gaze from Raul and threw her grandfather a perturbed look. "If you say so. Carl and I do a mean barbecue." There, that ought to show Raul that she already had a fiancé that would shield her from any of his attempts to frustrate her.

Raul changed the subject. "Do you mind if I ask you a personal question?"

"Not at all," Paloma answered lightly, placing a generous helping of tamales on his plate, the spicy tomato sauce splashing onto his hand.

Again their eyes connected. With a cynical smile turning his mouth, he asked, "Why would you take up plumbing and heating as a career?"

Paloma's grandfather leaned his head back and laughed. "That's my fault, I'm afraid." He held his crystal glass for Paloma to pour the spiced cherry wine over ice. "You see, Paloma's parents died just after she was born. Bad car accident." Pain was visible in his remembering.

"I'm sorry." Raul's light expression turned serious.

"No need. It was a long time ago. Not that I didn't love my daughter and her husband, but we still had Paloma. I don't know if we would have survived our grief without her."

She patted him on the arm. "That's right, but you were there for me too."

Mex turned his attention to Raul. "You see, from the time Paloma was a little *nina*, I took her to work with me. I taught her everything I knew. And I'm proud to say, next to me, she's the best in the business."

"Those are certainly excellent credentials, Mr. Espinoza."

"*Si.* Only because they're true. Anyone would be lucky to have Paloma on the job."

Paloma watched doubt creep into Raul's face. She knew why he didn't want her on the job and it had nothing to do with her qualifications. He had broken off their relationship a long time ago and he wanted to forget her. She would be an everyday reminder of what had happened between them.

"Do you like to fish?" Mex asked.

As Raul answered, Paloma's mind went off in another direction and didn't hear his comment, but she knew he liked to fish. They'd gone out on his friend's fishing boat many times that long ago summer.

She shoved the food around on her plate, having lost her appetite, which was a shame. Her grandmother was the best connoisseur of Mexican foods in the world. But tonight nothing tempted her, not even the mouth watering albondigas.

Dios, she was twenty-eight now. It was time she got on with her life and put Raul, their affair and the baby in the past. She would marry Carl and build a safe, secure, stable life with him. He was the one she chose to share her life with, to sit with on the porch in the evenings and enjoy the million dollar sunsets over Lake Michigan; someone to grow old with. One question, though, kept flashing through her mind: What about love?

Even though she told herself Carl was what she wanted, did she really love him in the way a man should be loved by the woman he married?

What about passion? Could she really have passion with Carl? It hadn't been part of their relationship up to now. What made her think it would be part of their marriage?

"Are you ready?" She jerked from her musings to her grandfather.

"What...? Ready...?" She threw a dazed glance from her grandfather to Raul.

"To go over the brochures and catalogues so Raul can pick out fixtures for the lodge. Weren't you listening?" her grandfather asked.

Warm color stained her face. "I guess I was daydreaming."

Her grandfather frowned. "I told Raul there are several designs in lavatory sinks he could choose from. And since they are custom designed, you'll have to get an order in as soon as possible."

"Right." Paloma pushed her untouched plate away.

"Aren't you going to eat? You haven't touched anything." Raul eyed the plate of untouched food.

"I'm just not hungry." Of course she wasn't hungry. Her appetite had been lost somewhere between his kissing up to her grandfather and those damned questions about love and passion which plagued her thoughts.

"Let's go into the den." Mex wheeled down the hall to the room opposite the living room. "I have several brochures and catalogues I'd like you to look at." Paloma rolled the double doors open as her grandfather navigated the room to the large mahogany desk.

"Nice." Raul glanced around the room that was very much a man's room, with its heavy furniture and dark paneling.

"This is Grandfather's home office." Paloma pulled out a chair so Raul could sit and go over the sink catalogue her grandfather had selected.

A high wind was picking up off Lake Michigan. The French doors creaked against the wind and the sheer curtains bounced this way and that. Paloma crossed the room in liquid movements and peered out into the stormy night.

"Grandfather loves his fresh air." She pulled the doors closed and latched them just as droplets began pelting the glass.

"Ah, rain. I understand the farmers are hoping for rain. It's been quite a dry spell," Mex said.

Paloma agreed. "I know, but with such a harsh winter and spring, I resent this cold rain. It might even turn to freezing rain before the night is over. After all, it was snowing this afternoon."

Mex shook his head. "It should be too late in the season for it to ice. But I do remember the ninth of May two or three years ago. The roads were coated with frozen slush until about noon."

"Give me the good ol' South," Raul answered.

"Is that where you're from?" Mex asked.

"From Florida, Little Havana. Originally I came North to pursue a career. Then when I first went into contracting, I took several contracts in the South. I like the moderate temperatures of course."

"I know what you mean." Mex nodded. "I've often thought about pulling up roots and moving back to Mexico now that I'm retired. But I have Paloma here to think about."

"Don't you worry about me." She turned from the torrent outside. "Carl will take good care of me. If you decide to move back to Mexico, you can be sure we will visit quite often." But her emotions belied her feelings. What would she do without the love and support of her grandparents?

Mex reached for the catalogues. "We might just as well get this meeting moving." He flipped the catalogue open.

Raul and her grandfather fell into an easy conversation about plumbing fixtures. Whenever Paloma offered advice, or Mex tried to bring her into the conversation, Raul easily dismissed her. She was once again in the roll of the little girl looking on, and she resented it.

She sat back on the green leather sofa, feeling out of sorts and very much out of place. Who did he think he was, ignoring her like this? She slumped further into the soft leather. She should be the one to handle the details of the job. Mex needed to worry about his health, not the job.

He was talking with Mex as an equal. But when he addressed her, he treated her as, what? Not a child exactly, but certainly as an inferior; as if she didn't have the mental capacity to grasp what he was saying.

Well, she wasn't going to sit back and let him get away with it. She was good at what she did. Damned good and before this job was done, he'd know just how good.

She glanced at her grandfather's pale and drawn face. He was doing too much. Pulling herself to all of her five-feet, three-inches, she squared her shoulders and marched over to the desk. "Pop, you look tired. Why don't you go rest? It's been a long day. I'll take it from here." She studied his pale complexion and strained expression.

Mex heaved a sigh and leaned back. "It's a long day, every day." He drew in a deep breath. "Where's the catalogue on customized sinks? I..." He glanced around, confusion etched in his face as he searched the top of his desk.

"It's right here." She patted the catalogue. "You're tired. Let me go over the fixtures with Raul." Paloma pulled the office chair to the desk. "You go upstairs and rest."

"I think you're right." Mex wheeled his chair away from the desk. "I'm sorry about this Raul, but this damned stroke has taken its toll on my health, I'm sorry to say. Listen to Paloma, my boy. She knows what she's talking about. Sometimes I think she knows more than I do now."

"I'll let you know what Raul has decided when I come up," she called out, turning the pages of the catalogue. "Here's a line of bathroom sinks you might like." She shoved a colorful catalogue toward Raul.

"Maybe I should wait until your grandfather feels better." He lifted himself easily from his chair.

Paloma threw him a scathing look. "He isn't going to get a whole lot better anytime soon. So let's get one thing straight right now. I'm running the plumbing, heating and air conditioning end of this project. You make the decisions on what you want and I'll take it from there." She was distracted for a moment as the motor on the stair elevator vibrated as it took her grandfather and his chair to the second floor.

"You don't mince words, do ya?" He dropped to his chair.

"I can't afford to. Look, Raul. I'm in business. I don't have time to fool around and play silly games. I'm good at what I do. Damned good. Pop saw to that. Now shall we get down to business?"

"I just thought it would be better if your grandfather and I talked this out, man to man. You can do the ordering."

"Look. He shouldn't have even invited you to dinner, much less discussed business. The doctor instructed him to have complete rest. He's retired. The business is mine to run as I see fit. If you deal with anyone, it will have to be me from now on. I won't risk his having another stroke because you'd rather deal with someone besides me."

For a few rocky moments the room was charged with heavy silence. Their eyes met, then Raul nodded curtly. "All right. Let me see the sink catalogue. I guess we could start there."

"Good idea." She shoved the opened catalogue to him. "These are china lavs with several different patterns around the edge. And as you can see, these are self-rimming."

He flipped through several pages. "So many designs to chose from."

"I know, but choosing is your job."

"Tell me about it," he grumbled. "This one will do, I think." He pointed to a lav that had simulated wear cracks in an oatmeal color.

"Are you going to put the same thing throughout the whole resort, or have different decors in various rooms?" She jotted notes on a small pad.

He glanced up. "I'm a builder, not an interior decorator."

"Maybe you should get one," she snapped, reaching for another brochure.

"I'm not so sure. You did a great job on this place, and I was thinking..."

"Are you actually asking that I give you advice in decorating this resort?"

"That's not a bad idea. The owners have given me total say in the completion of the whole project and I need a little help here. He wants the Timberline to be rustic. Nineteenth century rustic, like the days of the lumberjacks."

"Right. A few moments ago you couldn't see me for dust. Now all of a sudden you want my advice on decorating this whole thing?"

"Don't get your feathers ruffled. I'm used to working with men, that's all. I may come on a little strong at times. I'm sorry if I've hurt your feelings."

"Don't flatter yourself. But I am a professional and you've acted as if I don't exist, as if I don't know what I'm doing. And now you want my advice on decorating."

"I've apologized, what more do you want?"

"I'm a plumbing contractor and I'd like you to give me the respect I deserve, the respect I've earned over the years."

"You're a woman too and this place is going to need a woman's touch. So how about it?" He chose to ignore her scathing tongue.

"If you don't know a decorator, I'll suggest one." She reached for and grabbed several other larger catalogues, putting aside his request.

Raul leaned back, crossed his long, muscular legs and heaved a sigh. "You're going to make this hard on me, aren't you?"

"Hard?" Paloma tilted her head. "How so?"

"I don't know any decorators."

"I just said I'd get a list of them so you can chose one. Besides, you really don't want my help, now do you? You don't even want me on the site at all. After all, I'm a reminder of an unpleasant past." There, she'd said it. It was out in the open and the ball was in his court.

He gave a snort of angry defiance. "I wouldn't say the past was unpleasant. And I wouldn't have asked you if I hadn't wanted your help." He sat up as he spouted the words defensively.

Paloma saw slight color seep into his face and knew she'd hit a sore spot. "We might just as well get some things straight right now." She swallowed with difficulty and found her voice. "The past is in the past and I plan on keeping it there. I have a new life now. One that doesn't include you. But for the present, we're forced to work together, so let's make it as bearable as we can."

"I gave you a way out this afternoon, but you wouldn't take it."

"I can't afford to get out, as you put it. I need this job and plan to see it through to the end."

His expression softened and an awkward silence hung between them. "I am sorry. I never meant..."

Paloma raised her hand to stop him. "Let's stop bartering words and get down to business. Do you or don't you want the simulated cracked sinks ordered?"

"Yes. I want them. I also want gold fixtures." There was an edge of bitter cynicism in his voice.

Paloma was writing everything in her note book. "Here's a catalog on fixtures." She slid the catalogue across the desk without looking at him. "The polished brass are toward the back."

"Do you love him?"

Paloma jerked her head up, shock from his question settling around her. "What?"

"Do you love him?"

"Love who?"

"The man you're going to marry. This Carl fella? Do you love him?"

Paloma frowned. "That's a stupid question."

"Not so stupid. Simple is more the word. Do you?"

"We're discussing business, not my personal life. Now, let's get back to the fixtures." She opened another catalogue.

"Question too personal, huh?" Mockery touched his lips.

She swallowed hard, trying to maintain control, but he was arousing old fears and uncertainties. "My personal life is my own and I don't care to discuss it with you."

"That tells me a lot." He took the colorful brochure and glanced at it.

Fear mingled with anger wrapped itself around Paloma's heart. Could he see something in her she hadn't wanted to see herself? Oh, who was she trying to kid? She'd just as good as asked herself those same questions at dinner.

Raul uttered a sarcastic laugh. "I wonder how fast he'd marry you if he knew you didn't love him."

Paloma's face turned as hot as the anger she felt. "That's enough!" she snapped. "He's more man than you ever were or ever will be. He's dependable and loyal and..."

"Those are great reviews if I ever heard 'em, but they sound more like attributes you'd give a dog than to the man you're going to marry. I sure hope the woman I marry doesn't feel about me that way."

She was stunned and taken aback. Marry? He wasn't married now? What happened? Where was his wife? "You're not married?"

"Divorced."

"Oh, I'm sorry."

"Don't be. It was over a long time ago."

She shrugged. "I don't think you have to worry about getting married again. No one in her right mind would have you," she threw out before she could call back the words.

"You did...once."

Paloma scraped back her chair and sprung to her feet. "Just like you to throw up the past. But remember one thing, buster, you were the rat in our relationship. Now I think it's time to call it a night."

He rose abruptly. "Rat? Me?" He pointed at his chest and bent over her. "I was the one who came home from work to find you and everything you owned gone. There was just that stupid note saying not to try to find you, that you would be all right and our relationship was over. Rat? You tell me who was the rat."

She placed her hands on her hips. "You. You got two women pregnant at the same time. Did you think I wouldn't find out about Helena? Or did you plan to have a polygamous relationship with both of us?"

"She came to see you?"

"Of course. And to tell me the two of you were going to have a baby."

"*Dios.* I didn't know."

"Well, you know now and it doesn't make any difference." She handed him several brochures. "You take these home and study them. You can let me know tomorrow what you want."

He reached out for them. "I'll take these catalogues with me. I'll let you know in the morning exactly what sinks and fixtures I want."

He turned and slowly made his way from the room. Paloma watched his retreat. Something was wrong. He was really shocked at what she'd said.

No matter how Paloma tossed and turned in her bed trying to find a comfortable spot, sleep eluded her. Tomorrow was a big day. The undergrade at the Timberline had to be finished and she had to order material for two other jobs that were ready to go.

But the job wasn't what kept her awake. Thoughts of Raul ran through her brain. He was the most insufferable, chauvinistic, egotistical man she'd ever met. Just who did he think he was? God's gift to women? No, he thought he owned the world and everyone in it. *Dios,* what an insufferable bore he was. She glanced at the clock. One o'clock. If she didn't get to sleep soon, she wouldn't be good for anything tomorrow. Forget Raul and think pleasant thoughts. Oh, sure, like what? He'd brought up all sorts of memories and opened old wounds. How was she supposed to sleep?

Reaching for her robe, Paloma threw her legs over the bed. She was drawn to the closet. Slowly she rose and moved toward the door. After pulling the chain to the light, she reached for the box that had stayed against the back wall, untouched for several months. After seeing Raul today, she had this intense need to touch the items from her past.

She sat in the white wicker rocker holding, almost cradling the cardboard shoe box. It had been years since she'd looked into it. She'd only opened it once a year, on

February 11th, to place a card inside. She'd been strong...until now.

A draft of wind hit her bedroom windows. The shutters groaned under the pressure of its force as the storm raged, just as a storm of emotions ravaged Paloma's heart. She studied the box. She should just put it back, forget it. But of course she couldn't. Damn, why did he have to come back and dredge up the past?

Paloma's heart constricted as she lifted the lid with shaking hands. Her fingers lightly touched the small plastic tag that read, Baby Girl Ortega. She remembered begging the nurse to hold her baby just once before signing her away. It was then she'd taken the tiny band from the baby's leg and slipped it into her robe pocket.

She could still feel the silky wisps of dark hair atop the baby's head. Inside the plastic bag were fine dark hairs; hairs that she had secretly clipped from her baby.

She could still smell the sweet, baby smell of the tiny bundle she'd cradled in her arms, hear how her daughter had cried and sucked greedily on her tight little fist, until the nurse came to take her away.

These emotions were all-consuming. She thought she had put this behind her, had gotten on with her life and now the memories came flooding back as if everything had happened yesterday. She knew she had done the right thing. She hadn't been able to tell her grandparents what had happened. It would have broken their heart to know she'd had a child without the benefit of marriage, much less given it up for adoption.

Her grandparents were strict and old-fashioned. She hadn't wanted to disappoint them. And she hadn't been able to supply the child with a two-parent family it rightly deserved. The only sensible thing to do had been to give the baby up to a loving family with both a mother and a father.

Where was her daughter now? What did she look like? Did she look like her with brown eyes, or did she have her father's black eyes and winning smile? Was she happy? Did she have everything she wanted? Did she ever think about her birth mother? Ever wonder about her at times? Did she even know she was adopted?

Beneath the bracelet lay a gold chain, the chain Raul had given her when they'd moved into their apartment together. She picked up the expensive piece of jewelry. Not in eleven years had she looked at it, much less touched it. But now, Raul had opened all the wounds, all the old memories, good and bad.

She held both the plastic bracelet and the gold chain against her lips. Tears of pent-up sorrow spilled down her face. Somewhere out there was a young girl who was her daughter. And somehow she was going to find out about her.

Closing the box, she returned it to the shelf, slipped back into bed and pulled the quilts tightly under her chin. Somewhere between thinking about Raul and thinking about their child, she slipped into a restless sleep, haunted by dreams of Raul, their passionate lovemaking which had created the most beautiful baby in the world.

❦

Her eyes flew open and she glanced at the clock. Five-thirty. A hot shower, that's what she needed, a hot shower to wash Raul from her mind.

When she stepped from the shower and slipped on her white terry robe, the phone was ringing.

"Hello?" she answered breathlessly.

"Paloma? Is that you?"

"Of course it's me."

"Is anything wrong? You sound out of breath."

"Nothing's wrong. I just rushed to answer the phone." She pulled the robe more tightly around her body as if Raul could see her.

"What do you want, Raul?" she spoke into the receiver.

"My furnace is out. It's getting cold in here."

"So? Call a furnace man."

"I just did. How soon can you come and fix it?"

Paloma heaved a sigh. Just what she needed right now. "I'll send one of the guys to look at it. What's your address?"

"Afraid to come yourself?" The mocking voice taunted her.

She ignored his baiting. "I have a lot of things to do."

"Yes, and one of them is to fix my furnace. Come on, show me just how good you are."

That prickled. He was goading her and she knew it, but she couldn't let him get away with it. "All right. I'll grab a bite and come right over. What's your address?"

He gave her his address and said, "Never mind breakfast. I have the coffee on. You can have a bite with me."

Chapter Three

"Now, what seems to be wrong with your furnace?" Paloma set the tool caddy down and removed her denim jacket while glancing around the country kitchen of the spacious log home. The smell of frying bacon and fresh coffee made her mouth water.

Raul shrugged as he turned the thick, sizzling bacon. "I don't know. It won't run."

Paloma frowned. "I guessed that. But do you have any idea what's wrong? Did it make any strange sounds before it stopped? Any bangs or poofs? Did you forget to pay your gas bill maybe?" The words slipped from her lips before she could recall them.

"Very funny." Raul threw a frown in her direction. "It just stopped running and won't start."

"Did you press the restart button. You know, the little red one on the side of the motor?"

"I know where it is. And yes, I pressed it. Nothing happened."

"Well, I'll take a look at it." She picked up the caddy and followed him down the steps into a recreational basement with a pool table and complete entertainment center. For someone here for so short a time, he'd made himself right at home. The whole basement was paneled in diagonal pine. Indirect lighting from an extended ceiling and cream-colored Berber carpet gave a soft glow to the whole room. Colorful Navajo rugs used for accent contributed a Southwestern touch.

Inside the utility room at the far end of the basement, Paloma removed the jacket door of the furnace. She lifted the cast iron fire pot door and checked the pilot. No pilot. No gas. But everything seemed in working order, She pressed the reset button. Nothing. Not even a spark from the electric igniter. "The pilot's out. You know, this is a brand new furnace. It's still under warranty. You should have called the installer." She glanced up from her uncomfortable position.

"Don't worry, I'll pay you."

"Darned right you will." She stooped and crouched on her knees to looked back into the furnace.

"Strange," Raul said, watching her every move. "Maybe a wind from the right direction blew the pilot out. It was from the northwest last night."

"This is a pretty expensive joke." Her lips thinned in irritation as she observed the grin he was trying to control. "You know you called me out on gold time?"

"Something must be wrong with the furnace," he said innocently.

"There's nothing wrong with this furnace that turning it on wouldn't cure." She reached to the side of the motor and snapped on the switch. "Now I'll light the pilot and be on my way. I have more things to do than play your childish games." She glanced in his direction. He stood with his back against the door, his legs apart, his arms folded across his chest. His blue eyes bored into hers.

He tried to coax her into a better mood by saying, "I thought a little humor might lighten our situation. I mean, we parted on strained terms last night."

"Very funny." She reached into the furnace with the long metal match lighter to light the pilot. "I have a lot of work to do and a lot of business to take care of. I don't have time for this," she said, clearly annoyed. She refused to allow him to believe she was in any way amused by his prank.

"How about a little breakfast before you go?"

"I don't think so." She put her tools back neatly into the caddy.

"Surely you have time for coffee," he prompted.

She straightened to her full height and faced him. "Look, yesterday you were doing your darndest to get rid of me. Now you want to have breakfast together and for me to become your interior decorator. I don't understand you. Just what do you want from me?"

Raul held out his hand. "Let's call a truce, okay?"

"Why should I?" She stared at his outstretched hand. Oh no, he couldn't win her over with his tricks and smooth talk. An icy anger rose inside her at his chicanery.

He shot her an ironic smile. "Because I've changed my mind. I've examined the work you've already done. It's good and I apologize for suggesting you would do any less than excellent work."

His sudden change in attitude threw her off balance. The way he looked at her caused old memories to come rushing back. Memories best forgotten. She reached down and lifted the caddy, her jaw set in determination as she moved toward the rustic stairs. The carpet muffled her angry steps.

"You haven't given me an answer yet," Raul called after her.

She stopped in mid-step and squeezed her eyes tight. What in heaven's name did he want from her? Was he trying to get his pound of flesh? He was the one who walked out of their relationship, not her. If he was trying to unnerve her, he was doing a pretty good job of it. Slowly she turned to face him, cocked her head, heaved a deep sigh and said, "What answer? Am I going to stay for breakfast, or am I ready to accept your truce?"

"Both." He moved toward her and fingered a soft tendril that wisped about her face. "You're not afraid to have breakfast with me, are you?"

She jerked away, her back ramrod straight, her stance tense—though her heart beat like a butterfly trapped inside a closed window. He wasn't going to give up easily. For some reason he was reverting to his old lighthearted teasing, shedding the cloak of hardness.

She lifted her gaze to his and fought not to drown in that remembered warmth. She swallowed hard. "You should know I'm not afraid of anything." That was a lie. She had become afraid of a lot of things since the end of their relationship. Afraid her grandparents would find out she'd had an affair. Afraid they'd find out about the baby. Afraid Raul would find out and hate her for giving their child away as much as she hated herself for it.

"I guess I have time for a quick coffee." She knew she shouldn't, but what would one cup hurt? Besides, she'd left home without the benefit of her morning caffeine.

"Good, it's all ready." He followed her up the steps, so close she could feel his warm breath against her neck. Shoving the tingling sensation aside, she pulled away from him and walked across the kitchen to the door.

Paloma put her caddy outside on the rustic deck and returned to the kitchen. She noted the fine hand-crafted oak cupboards in early American styling, and the almond appliances and sink.

"Do you rent this place?"

Raul stood at the stove with his back to her. "Yep. I got a deal too." He stirred onions and green peppers into the eggs and slowly poured them into the already hot cast iron skillet. He next handed her a steaming brown mug of coffee. "Have a seat." He motioned to the round oak table with matching chairs.

"I really can't stay." She sipped the reinforcing coffee.

"I'm fixing your eggs just the way you like them." He slowly turned the yellow mass until it was cooked, then put half on each plate, along with crispy pieces of bacon.

"I really shouldn't." Her gaze dropped to the picture-perfect breakfast. Her mouth watered and her stomach protested waiting any longer for food.

"Everything is just as you like it." He placed the plates on the table and seated himself.

Paloma was torn. She wanted to refuse, but part of her wanted to stay. Besides, she was starving. "All right, but then I really must go."

The toaster made a terrible rattling sound like hers did when toast got stuck.

"Oh, I forgot." Raul rose and took the golden toast from the toaster and buttered it. "Homemade." He held up the two pieces proudly.

Paloma drew her fine brows together. "You made homemade bread?" Her voice was shaky and that made her more angry. She didn't want to seem weak or nervous around him.

"Sure did," he nodded, then colored slightly. "Well, actually the breadmaker did."

Paloma laughed in spite of herself. "They're something, aren't they? We got Grandmother one for Christmas. Now we have homemade bread every day." She tried to keep her voice light and even, which wasn't easy with the confusion he brought out in her.

"How're your eggs?" he asked, motioning to her plate.

"Eggs?" She hadn't touched them. She picked up her fork and took a small bite. "Delicious." The bacon and eggs hit the spot, as did the toast with strawberry jam.

"Did you notice I never forgot your advice?"

"What advice?" she asked.

"The cast-iron skillet? Remember? You said not to waste my money buying those non-stick things, that if I'd just learn to use the cast iron, it would last me a lifetime?"

Paloma smiled, remembering their discussion of cookware. How times had changed. Years and circumstances had separated them and what they once felt for each other, but here they were, eating breakfast and chatting as if it were the most natural thing in the world. "I was right, wasn't I?"

"Who taught you about cookware?"

"Grandmother, of course. She wouldn't use anything else. Her mother taught her the old ways from Mexico and she clings to them religiously."

Raul finished the last of his toast and washed it down with his coffee. "More?"

"A little, then I really must go."

He went to the stove and brought the pot to the table. "Think it will warm up soon? It's darn cold for April."

"I don't know. This winter has been like the old days, so Grandfather says." But her mind wasn't on the deep snow that fell during the long, hard winter. She wasn't thinking about the times she wished for spring and the warmth of the summer sun. She was thinking about Raul and their child.

"I never expected to see you again." The words slipped from her mouth before she could stop them.

"Same here," he said, his voice low and smooth.

Paloma envisioned him together with his wife, perhaps raising a family. He said they were divorced. The child? Was it a boy or girl? Was there more than the one? What would he think if he knew he had another child out there somewhere?

"Penny for your thoughts," he broke in.

"Oh," she laughed nervously, "I was just lost in thought, that's all." She reached for her jacket. "I must go."

"But you haven't finished your coffee yet." He motioned to the cup.

She picked it up and gulped the liquid. "There, it's finished."

Rising, he took the dishes and flatware to the sink. "We do have things to say to each other, you know."

Paloma pulled her jacket on. "I think things are best left unsaid."

"Are you afraid to talk to me? After all, we shared a lot...for a while."

Paloma raised her hands to stop him. "I can't listen to this. I have another life for myself, a life with a good man. I won't jeopardize that."

"No one asked you to. I simply asked you to listen to me, to listen to my side of the story."

"You sound bitter," Paloma couldn't help saying.

He turned pained eyes to her. "I am bitter. Bitter for all the years I've lost because of her. Bitter because I lost..."

Paloma raised her hand to stay his comment. "I don't think we'd better get into this. The past is the past."

"Something is bugging you. Bugging you bad. And it has to do with me. Why not get it out in the open and deal with it."

Damn him! He had the slickest way of throwing the ball in her court.

He continued before she could answer. "You blame me for what happened. For some reason you think I walked out on you. I was the one stunned when you had left without telling me where you were going."

"Raul, I said I don't to talk about this."

"But I do."

"I don't have to listen to this." She looked up sharply and made to leave, but he stepped in front of her, blocking her retreat. She didn't want to listen. Bringing up the past would serve no purpose. It was over. Their affair was over.

"I loved you more than life itself. It tore me apart to come back and find you gone, to find that note. You never gave me a chance to tell you anything. You just took Helena's word that I wanted out of our relationship. Is that it? She told you I wanted to break up with you, didn't she?"

She wanted to leave, to be anywhere but here, but his gaze held her like a magnet. "You're going to insist we discuss the past, aren't you?"

"It's festering inside you, I can see it. A lot happened you don't know or understand."

"It's too late now." She tried to go around him. "We can't change the past." To her dismay, her voice wavered slightly.

"I know," he admitted. "We both have built new lives. But I think if we're going to work together we should try to put our anger behind us."

She searched his eyes. What was she hoping to see? Perhaps some flicker that she might still mean something to him? This was crazy! They were two very different people now. "Yes, new lives," she repeated.

Something flashed in his eyes, something strong and dangerous. Were there some feelings left for her after all? But what did it matter if he did have feelings? She was going to marry Carl. There was no place in her life for Raul. He was the past. What happened between them was a long time ago.

"I know. I hope you're..." His words were cut short by the shrill ringing of the old-fashioned phone above the butcher block. "I've got to answer that. Don't go away." He reached for the phone.

Paloma studied him as he answered it. His face was grim, the muscles in his face turned to stone. "What do you want from me now?"

Who was he talking to? Paloma wondered as she took the coffee cups to the sink. She rinsed the dishes and placed them in the dishwasher as Raul talked on the phone. She should leave. She felt like an eavesdropper listening to his angry words.

"If you want more money, I suggest you talk to your lawyer."

Was that Helena demanding money? she wondered.

He raked his fingers through his thick hair and his nostrils flared angrily. "What do you mean, he's my kid?"

Her heart constricted. Now she knew he had a son.

"You want me to take him? After the hell you put me through to take him away from me, you want me to have him now? Why?" He drew in a ragged breath and listened to the voice at the other end of the line. His face paled. "What kind of bitch are you?" Paloma stood transfixed. If looks could kill, the look on Raul's face would kill for ten miles in any direction. He was angry. No, not angry, mad. Fighting mad. She'd never seen him like this before.

"You're saying Rick is my son, my flesh and blood? If that's true, then why did you always say he wasn't?" He shook his head and closed his eyes as if the pain was too much to bear. "I don't know what kind of game you're playing, but I'm going to get to the bottom of this once and for all!" He hesitated, listening, then said, "Yes, dammit, I'll come get him, but you'll never see him again. My lawyers will see to that."

Again he listened to the unseen voice. "I said I'd come get him, didn't I? And you can bet your cheap life you won't ever get your greedy hands on him or my money again. I'll be leaving just as soon as I can. Have him ready." He slammed down the receiver.

Paloma didn't know what to do. Should she go or stay? He needed someone right now, that was obvious by the state he was in. But did he need her? Did he want her? She turned to leave.

"Paloma?"

"Yes?" She turned to him.

"Don't go. Not yet. Please."

"I don't know. I don't think I should..."

"I've got to talk to someone," he said.

"You want to tell me about it?" Paloma reluctantly moved to the table and sat down where she had eaten breakfast. He had a son! The knowledge was like salt in her open wounds. She had a child too. A daughter who was beautiful, perhaps with her father's black hair. God, how she wanted to see her. Raul broke in on her troubled thoughts.

"I love Rick. I've always loved Rick," he said in an unnaturally vulnerable voice. Raul joined her at the table. "Helena always told me I wasn't the father. Now, out of the blue, she tells me to come get him, that I am his biological father."

"Does it really matter?" she asked softly. "If you were there to raise him, he's your son, blood or not." Paloma felt angry at Helena for what she'd put him through. No wonder he looked so beaten, so soured on life. He had as much to be angry and upset about as she did.

"Anyway," his voice broke in on her thoughts, "I wanted to tell you about Rick."

She stiffened, torn by conflicting emotions. "You don't owe me any explanations..."

Raul studied her. "Am I wrong in feeling animosity between us?"

"Raul, I don't know what you want from me. I can't tell you how many times I've said the past is the past. Why keep rehashing it?"

"You should have confided in me, have trusted me..."

She swallowed hard. "I did what I thought was best...best for us both."

"Do you want me to salve your conscience? Do you want me to say I wasn't hurt? That I completely understand and accept what happened? Well, I can't. I was hurt. I expected you to come back, to write, to call me for God's sake, but you didn't."

"Raul, I..." He was throwing the blame on her. Had she done the wrong thing? Should she have waited and listened to him before she left?

Their gazes locked and time slipped away as the past surfaced. He reached out and cupped her face. She trembled as he lowered his lips to hers.

With every ounce of strength she had, Paloma fought the slow exquisite pleasure of his touch. "Raul..."

Ignoring her protest, his lips moved across hers. "This is for old times' sake." His arms tightened around her soft body and pulled her close.

Time stood still. Unable to deny Raul, unable to deny her own needs, she gave herself up to his kiss. His tongue slipped between the satin of her lips and out again. Every nerve in her body tingled in sensual pleasure. The rest of the world drifted away as she and Raul dove deeper into flames of passion.

No, her mind kept warning, but her body betrayed what she knew was right.

"Oh, sweet Paloma," he whispered against her lips.

Warning bells sounded again. Good Lord, they were only alone for a few moments and she'd nearly lost it. Nearly, nothing. She'd lost it. What was it about him that captivated her so? Hadn't she learned the first time around?

She pushed against his chest. "No! I can't do this. It's all wrong."

Raul slowly released her, a crooked smile touching his mouth. "It didn't seem very wrong a few moments ago."

An interrupting knock at the door stopped further conversation. He glanced at Paloma. Their gazes locked for several moments, then Raul broke the spell by turning to answer the persistent second knock.

"Carl." Raul stepped back, swinging the cross-buck door wide open.

"Carl." Paloma steadied herself by gripping the back of the chair, her heart pounding in her ears. "What are you doing here?" Why had he come now, at this precise moment? Good Lord, could he see from the flush in her face she had just been in Raul's arms, experienced the most sensual kiss she'd had in twelve years?

"I heard from one of the guys you called and said Raul was having trouble with the furnace and you'd be a little late. I came to see if I could help." He glanced from Raul to Paloma as if he could feel the strained atmosphere.

"No, I was just leaving." Paloma forced a smile she didn't feel. "The furnace is fixed and I was just having a cup of coffee."

Paloma was caught in her half-lie when Carl's gaze fell to the table void of cups.

"What was wrong with it?" he asked.

"The pilot was out. I lit it." Paloma zipped up her jacket to keep her trembling fingers busy.

"Good." His brows narrowed into a slight frown as if puzzled by the tension-filled room. "Oh, and you know those special schedule 40 wyes? We're going to need them tomorrow. I guess I have to make a special trip to Traverse City to get some."

Paloma moved out onto the deck and turned to Raul. "I think the furnace will be all right now. There shouldn't be any more northwest winds this season."

Raul nodded. "Thanks for coming out. Send me a bill."

All the way back to the shop Paloma thought about her encounter with Raul. She tried to put him out of her mind by thinking about Carl, his dependability, his gusto for work and his...his what? Flare for life? He never exhibited any. But he was sturdy and dependable.

Carl followed close behind in his truck. They pulled into the shop together.

"Want to go to Traverse City with me?"

The question startled her. "Why? What are you going for?"

Carl looked at her and let out an exasperated sigh. "I already told you I had to make a run to get those wyes. Weren't you listening?"

Paloma felt embarrassing color stain her face. "Right. I remember. I've had my mind on other things." Did she ever. Like Raul's mouth, his kiss, and the feel of his arms around her. And the way her body responded to his touch.

Carl frowned. "Like the new general contractor perhaps? What's going on between the two of you?"

The question unnerved her. Had it been so obvious? "I don't know what you mean." She lowered her gaze so he wouldn't see her lie. "I don't even like this guy."

"Then why didn't you send one of the guys to fix that furnace? You didn't have to go yourself, unless you wanted to."

Paloma smiled blandly. "Why Carl Andrew, you sound jealous." She forced a teasing tone.

"Jealous? Me?" He lifted his brows in surprise. "You know me better than that. I trust you. There just seems to be something between you. I think I deserve to know what it is."

Paloma cleared her throat. "Raul and I knew each other a long time ago when I was a freshman in college. I knew his wife too." She told the half truth. "He was telling me they were divorced now, that's all."

It was a flimsy explanation, but strangely Carl brightened and seemed to accept it without question. No jealousy or need of further explanation.

"Well that explains it then. Do you want to come along?" Carl shed his denim jacket and threw it behind the seat in the truck.

"I don't know...I've got a lot to do here."

"Oh, come on," he urged. "It will do us good. Jim can handle the crew. We can have a day alone together."

Paloma knew what that meant. Carl was going after material and he would talk of nothing but work, the job and material. Well, that's what she wanted, wasn't it? Dependability, security, a down-to-earth, no-nonsense kind of guy. She'd certainly have it with Carl.

"All right. Give me five minutes with Jim and I'll be ready."

The trip to Traverse City was restful except for Carl's non-stop talk about the job and the ones that had yet to be bid. She talked about the jobs too when it was necessary, but Carl talked about work even when they were having a break.

She turned her thoughts away from his droning voice to the scenery outside. The shore drive was coming alive with springtime green. Lake Michigan had lost its gray-winter look and taken on the blue-green of summer. Whitecaps dotted the bay and rolled to shore as waves.

The cherry orchards would soon be blooming, the very orchards her grandfather had come North to pick so many years ago. She hoped to get Carl to the Cherry Festival this year. Fat chance. He thought festivals were a foolish waste of time.

"I have that Hanson job all figured and priced out. You can go over it when we get back and see if you see anything that needs to be changed." She loved working as much as he, getting a real sense of accomplishment when everything went like clock work. But on this day when they could be together and get closer, he wanted to talk shop.

They stopped at a little fast food place outside Traverse City for a cup of coffee and a bite to eat.

"It's a little cool, but let's sit outside at the tables." They picked up their coffee and breakfast sandwiches and moved outside.

"It is cool," Paloma agreed when they sat at the umbrella table. She pulled her jacket tightly around her against the unceasing wind.

"I've got a little surprise for you." Carl reached into his pocket and pushed a gray velvet box across the table toward her. "I picked it up from the jewelers yesterday."

Paloma opened the lid and there, nestled against white velvet, was a sparkling diamond in old-fashioned, white-gold filigree setting.

"Carl?" She lifted her gaze to his.

He grinned proudly. "It was my grandmother's. I thought you'd like to have it." He motioned to the box as he took a large bite of his sandwich. "Go on, try it on."

Paloma lifted her gaze to his. No romance. No bending on his knee and placing the token of his love on her finger. No longing looks exchanged between love-struck eyes. Just plain sensible, dependable Carl and his grandmother's engagement ring.

Paloma slipped the ring from the box and put it on her finger. It looked and felt strangely heavy and out of place. She lifted her gaze. There should be ringing bells and shooting stars, but there was just...what? Just nothing.

"So, I've been thinking," Carl said in between bits of his sandwich. "Since you got the ring, we might as well set the wedding date. What do you think?"

Finally, he had asked her what she thought. Wedding date. She glanced at the ring again. It was stunning and sparkled fire, but where was the romance? A ring this beautiful shouldn't be given in a fast food place. There should be moonlight and roses. Romance and passion, a candlelight dinner with soft music and a gentle fire simmering in a fireplace.

"Wedding date?"

"Yes. We might as well settle on a date and get it over with."

Get it over with? You only get married once in a lifetime, hopefully, and he wanted to get it over with? She was about to protest his timing, but what good would it do? Carl was Carl and always would be.

"I don't know," she said sullenly. "What did you have in mind?"

He shrugged. "It doesn't really matter to me, except the jobs usually slow up about January and I guess we could take a little time off then. How about January 15?"

"How about February 14?" she countered.

"Valentine's Day?" He pulled a face. "I don't think we should get all sloppy and gooey about this. I want it to be just like us. Sensible and orderly. So, what do you say? January 15?"

Paloma heaved a sigh. "January 15." She gazed at the ring that should have brought her happiness. But instead it brought her logic and stability. It also brought her a protection against Raul. Raul, who made her heart race a mile a minute; who lit a fire whenever he touched her. Was she ready to give all that up for logic and dependability?

Give it up! What was she thinking. She didn't have it. Raul threw her crumbs of the past. Here today and gone tomorrow. No, Carl was here forever.

Carl broke in on her thoughts. "Are you ready to go?"

"I'm ready. Would you mind stopping at the Grand Traverse Mall for a few minutes while we're here? There are a few things I'd like to pick up," she said as she slid into the truck.

Carl shook his head. "What's with you and that mall? I suppose you women are all alike. It's just one big buyer's trap, you know." He crossed traffic and drove toward the city.

Paloma sat silent, but her mind was racing. He never wanted to do the things she liked. Oh, yes he did. They had work in common.

"Coming?"

"What...?"

"We're here." He pointed to the large white building. "The supply house."

Once inside, Carl moved straight to the plumbing section and began sorting through the bin of fittings. While Carl picked out what he needed, Paloma's mind kept returning to Raul, his kiss, the feel of his muscled chest, the scent of his musky after-shave, his gentle teasing and lightheartedness.

Why did she have to be haunted by him on a day that should have been the happiest day of her life? The scent of his cologne filled the air so strongly she'd swear...

"Raul! What are you doing here?" she exclaimed, as she turned, coming face-to-face with her thoughts.

He pulled a wide grin. "I could ask you the same thing, but then, it's a small world, isn't it?"

Paloma turned her attention to the boy beside him who looked very much as Raul must have at the same age. He had dark laughing eyes and black hair just like his father's. How could Raul ever think this boy wasn't his son?

"Paloma, I'd like you to meet my son Rick." He put a hand on the boy's shoulder. "Rick, this is the plumbing contractor for the Timberland, Paloma Ortega."

"Hello Rick." Paloma held out her hand and Rick readily took it.

"Hi, Paloma."

Raul frowned. "Miss Ortega," he corrected.

"No, no, please," Paloma said. "You can call me Paloma. And this is Carl, my fiancé."

Carl moved in and placed a protective arm around Paloma. "And I'm pleased to say Paloma and I just settled on our wedding date. January 15. I'm sure I speak for Paloma when I say I hope you can come. It will be small, but binding."

There was a pregnant silence between them. Raul frowned as Carl held out Paloma's hand.

"It was my grandmother's. I had it sized for Paloma."

"I guess congratulations are in order," Raul offered, his expression anything but congratulatory. "How about letting me buy you lunch to celebrate. How about Boons restaurant? My treat."

"No—no, we couldn't." Paloma shook her head, frantically wanting to get away from this tight situation. She peered at him through heavy lashes. His expression was hard, twisting into a cynical, mocking smile. It crushed the air from her lungs, sending spirals of apprehension down her spine.

"Now, Paloma, let's not be hasty." Carl pulled her closer, as if protecting an investment. "Raul was kind enough to ask us out and I think we should accept."

"Of course you should. In fact, I insist," Raul said, a look of devilish amusement flashing in his eyes.

Chapter Four

Paloma tossed and turned in her bed for what seemed like hours. The trip from Traverse City was strained after the disastrous dinner at Boons. And there was no doubt in her mind what Raul had done. He had tried to make Carl look like a cold, unfeeling oaf by arranging their wedding for the slow time of the year, instead of letting the heart dictate the memorable day.

The fact that he had been right made her even angrier. And she was angrier still that Carl was blind to the whole thing. Or indifferent, which was worse.

She held up her left hand so the light from the bright, full moon caught the diamond's facets and made it sparkle like the brightest, coldest star in the velvety night. The ring and her engagement should have given her a warm sense of peace and security, but it didn't. There wasn't the happiness or joy that should be all-consuming during happy engagement days, only a cold emptiness.

What had she expected? After all, she and Carl had decided on the kind of relationship they wanted. They had work in common and both had an unyielding need to accomplish their work to perfection. Of course, it was true they had occasional good times, but mostly they were one when it came to their work.

Doubts nagged at the back of her mind. Had she settled too quickly for a substitute for passion and romance.

Oh, she knew all about passion. She'd shared that period of her life with Raul and look where it got her. Would she spend the rest of her life regretting the loss of her relationship with Raul?

She wouldn't have given her relationship with Carl a second thought if Raul hadn't barged into their well-arranged lives, turning everything upside down. She threw back the covers and went to the closet. She turned on the light and stared at the box on the shelf. Slowly she reached for it, closed her eyes and clutched it to her chest.

Tears burned in her eyes. Of course if she were honest she'd have to admit there were times that she'd thought about Raul and their baby. She couldn't help thinking about them at times. They had been an important part of her life. But for eleven years she'd kept a level head on her shoulders and kept her emotions under control. And now she felt like crumbling at the first sign of a crisis.

As she sat in the white wicker rocking chair holding her box of memories, she thought about her child. Raul's child. There was no time to waste. She must find her. Carl would help her when he found out. After all, he loved her, didn't he?

"You what?" Carl sat behind the steering wheel of his pickup, his head resting on it.

"I'm sorry." Paloma whispered, watching his hands tighten on the wheel. "I should have told you a long time ago. But I hadn't counted on needing to find my child this badly."

Carl hit the steering wheel with the palm of his hand. "Why now, after all this time? What's made you so obsessed with finding her now?" He swore under his breath. "Who's the father anyway? Do I know him?"

Twisting her fingers together nervously, she asked, "Does it matter? I just need to find my daughter...for me. I have to know she's okay. I need to know she's happy and has two parents who love her. I'm not planning to bring her into our lives. I wouldn't do that to her or to you."

If the truth be told, she'd give her right arm to have her daughter with her. To tell her how much she loved her. How much she'd always loved her. But of course, that was asking too much. She'd have to be satisfied with the knowledge her daughter was a happy, well-adjusted child.

"Yeah, right, but you can throw this little bit of information in my lap and expect me to like it," he sneered, an angry side of him appearing that Paloma had never seen before.

"I had to be honest with you." She fought the anger that surged through her. "This has nothing to do with you anyway. I'm just sharing a piece of my life with you, that's all. A piece of my life that happened long before I ever met you."

He threw her a dark, scathing look void of understanding. "Okay, let's say you locate your daughter. What then? What good is that going to do?"

"I would be satisfied with the knowledge that she's all right. That she's happy and loved."

"That's stupid. Of course she's loved. Who would be crazy enough to adopt a kid they didn't love?" Carl raked his fingers through his hair. "Just forget it! We have a life to live. A life to build together. There's no room in it for this bastard kid of yours."

Shock surged through her, fanning her heated hurt and anger. Bastard child? He'd called her baby a bastard? She felt as if she'd been hit in the stomach full force. Fighting for control she drew in a ragged breath. Carefully and deliberately slow, Paloma turned to face him. Slipping the engagement ring from her finger she handed it to him.

"Then I think this belongs to you." Her voice was stern with no vestige of forgiveness in its hardness.

"Hey, Paloma, come on. Be reasonable," he beseeched, staring at the ring. "This has been a shock, you know? How did you expect me to react?" His attitude took a ninety degree turn.

"Like you really loved me and would stand beside me no matter what. Like you might understand what I'm going through. What I've been through for the past eleven years."

"Paloma, I didn't create this situation. You did."

"Exactly. I created it and I'll solve it myself." She opened the truck door and slid to the ground, slamming it behind her. Where she was going she had no idea but it had to be away from Carl. As far away from him as possible.

This was a stupid thing to do, to step out into the dark night so far from town, but fury knew no logic. The construction site was deserted. And she'd come with Carl. Behind her the truck door opened and slammed. Then, determined footsteps.

"Paloma, be reasonable. We have too much to throw it all away. Think about me. How I feel. If you really loved me, you wouldn't ask me to take another man's kid."

"I never asked you to take my daughter. I simply told you about a part of my life and that I needed to know she was all right and you jump to absurd conclusions."

Carl's face turned red. "That's the way things start out, but I know women. You'll find her and then get this damned nesting thing women always get around children and the next thing you know, you'll want to bring her into our home."

She felt her temper raise in response. Anger anew traveled up her spine. "I'm not asking you anything. Not any more. What we had is over. Done with. Finished." She threw up her hands in disgust.

He strode toward her. Grabbing her by the shoulders, he said, "Give this thing up. Think about us, our future. You can't do this to us."

She jerked away. "We don't have a future. You can finish this job with me and then you'd better find yourself another job."

"You don't mean that. Paloma, think..." His tone suddenly changed to one of appeal.

She backed away. She didn't need to think about it. He'd forced her into it by his reaction to what she'd told him. He wasn't the kind of man she wanted to spend the rest of her life with.

She'd already told him she only wanted to find out about her daughter, not intrude on her life. She just had to find out if she was all right. If her family loved her. But Carl couldn't understand that, he'd just made that abundantly clear.

"Paloma. Let's start this conversation again. I'm sure I came across the wrong way." He reached toward her.

"You got that right." She backed away from him. There was no way she was going to allow him to touch her now. He'd made his feelings known. No matter how hard he tried, he couldn't take back those hateful, ugly words.

"Does your grandfather know about this baby and who the father is."

He seemed to be waiting for her to crumble, to find a crack in her control. Although fear gripped her heart like an icy hand, she was determined to show him how unconcerned she was about his subtle threat. But she had forgotten about Mex. He couldn't learn about her baby until she had the chance to tell him herself, when the time was right. There was no way she'd let Carl tell her grandfather. It would be too much of a shock. It might even throw him into another stroke.

"Of course, he knows," she lied smoothly. "And I don't think he'd appreciate your attitude about it either." She saw uncertainty gather in his eyes as he assessed her. He wasn't so sure now. Doubt stretched between them. If she could stall Carl from making a scene until tomorrow, her grandparents would be gone to the Upper Peninsula cabin for a while.

"I'm tired of talking, Carl. Please, just go home and leave me alone."

"I think we have to discuss this. We can't end our relationship like this."

She shook her head. "Not tonight. I'm tired. I can't talk about this any more."

"Come on. Be reasonable. Get in the truck. How you gonna get home?" He walked forward, stopping in front of her.

"I don't know," she snapped. "I'll walk if I have to."

"Don't be stupid. It's a good ten miles to your house. Let me take you home."

"No," she hissed. "Just leave me alone." In a defiant gesture she folded her arms over her chest and began walking to the trailer that served as Raul's office. Perhaps he'd left it unlocked. If he had, she could call a taxi.

"Paloma," Carl called, holding out the ring. "Please take it back. At least for tonight. We can talk after you've calmed down."

"I'm not going to calm down," she threw over her shoulder. "As far as I'm concerned, if I never see you again, it will be too soon."

Heavy footsteps pounded their way behind her. Carl grabbed her and swung her around none too gently. "You can't do this to me."

"I'm not doing anything to you," she said softly. "But I want you to take your hands off me."

"Think about the business. You need me. Do you honestly think you can run a crew of men without me?" His voice turned hard and angry.

Paloma jerked her shoulders from his grasp. "So, that's it. You're afraid of losing the business. A business my grandfather built from the ground up. My business."

"There you go, being foolish and emotional again."

It was a good thing she'd found out how selfish and self-centered he really was. What a mess this would be if they were married. She shook her head. "It's over. Nothing you can say will change that."

"You think not?" He reached out and roughly grabbed her again, his mouth coming down on hers, bruising her tender lips.

"Carl, please. Let me go." She twisted against his hold but anger and strength outweighed her.

"You play the high and mighty lady, saving yourself for our wedding night, and then you turn out to be nothing but a common tramp." His mouth covered hers again.

"Carl, you're hurting me." She squirmed against his bulk.

"I'll do more than hurt you. I just might take what you've denied me but saw fit to give to another. God, how stupid I've been." He grabbed the front of her jacket and yanked it open so hard he broke the zipper.

Fear gripped her heart. He couldn't do this. Not the man she'd been going to marry. Not the one person she thought she could trust with anything, including her life.

He threw her roughly to the ground, ripping her blouse. Then he was over her, his hands pinning her to the ground.

"Let the lady go!" A deep, familiar voice edged with danger cut through the darkness.

"What the..." Carl dropped his hands from Paloma's shoulders.

"I said, let the lady go." Raul sauntered from the shadows of the piled logs and into the brilliant moonlight.

"What are you doing here?" Carl demanded, visibly shaken by the unexpected intrusion.

"Does it matter?" Raul reached down and helped Paloma to her feet. "I think it's time you left."

"See here, this is none of your business. This is between Paloma and me."

"Is that so?" Raul turned his eyes toward Paloma. "Do you want me to leave?"

"No. I want Carl to leave." She rubbed her mouth with the back of her hand, feeling like a senseless dolt. She'd always prided herself on being able to take care of herself and here she was, allowing Raul to play hero to her maiden in distress predicament.

Tears gathered in her eyes. Who was she trying to kid? If Raul hadn't shown up when he had, Carl would have forced himself on her.

"Stay out of this," Carl warned indignantly, the nostrils of his nose flaring angrily, his breathing heavy and ragged.

Paloma stepped back as Carl advanced toward them, his fists raised, ready to do battle. His dark face was set in a vicious expression, his mouth twisted in anger.

"Go home and cool off." Raul stepped back. "I don't want to fight you."

Paloma knew Raul didn't want to fight Carl but Carl wasn't going to give in, that was obvious by his determined stance. He stepped close and took a swing with his right fist, just missing Raul's chin. Raul avoided a second thrust and this time his own fist struck out and connected. In just a matter of seconds Carl lay sprawled on the construction sand.

"Go cool off. I'll see Paloma home." Raul reached out to help Carl to his feet.

Carl struggled to his feet, jerking away from Raul's hand. He rubbed his chin and looked at the stain of blood that came from his mouth. "You'll regret this, greaser. By God, you'll both regret it." He backed away in uneven steps.

Paloma and Raul watched him stumble into the darkness. Then the sound of his engine springing to life. The truck roared away. The sound of spinning tires spewing gravel cut through the night.

"Come into the office. I think there's some hot coffee left." Raul gently took her elbow and urged her toward the darkened trailer.

"What are you doing here this late?" she asked, her voice just a faint whisper.

"I had some paperwork to catch up on. What are you doing here?" he asked.

"Carl forgot his mortar saw and we came to pick it up. "I've never seen him like this." Her voice was shaky.

"What happened to set him off like that? Or maybe I shouldn't ask."

Paloma didn't answer right away. Thoughts raged through her brain. Her life had just taken a complete turnaround. Just when you think you have things all figured out, you find you don't, she thought.

Raul placed the key into the lock, reached inside and flicked on the light, spreading a warm, inviting glow over the small office.

"Black, right?" He handed her the mug he'd just filled with the last of the coffee.

"Thanks." She sat in the leather chair, letting the hot coffee do its work.

Raul sat in the chair opposite, concern written on his face. "Are you sure you're all right?"

Paloma nodded her head. "I'm fine. Really."

"Just relax a few minutes and I'll take you home."

Strange. She had made up her mind to settle for the security Carl offered. His actions tonight showed her there was more than the lack of romance in their relationship. He was a very selfish, self-centered oaf with a temper to match. He wasn't the gentle person she'd thought him to be. There was another side of him she'd never known existed.

As the unexpected relief enveloped her, she realized she could now concentrate on finding her daughter without deterrence from anyone. She could go to Kalamazoo and see the adoption lawyer who had made all the arrangements eleven years ago. The Timberland project was well enough along that it didn't need her constant oversight.

"I'll go to Kalamazoo, that's what I'll do," Paloma whispered, staring into space.

"Kalamazoo?" Raul asked, studying her hypnotic musing.

Paloma jerked her head up as if surprised to see him sitting across from her. She lifted her chin, wiped the tears from her eyes and nodded. "Yes, Kalamazoo. This job is coming along nicely and I can take a few days off. I have some personal business to attend to."

"How long are you going to be gone?"

"Not long. At least I don't think I'll be gone for very long. I should be back by the end of the week." Carl should be able to handle everything. But could she trust him? He might deliberately botch things up because of their disagreement. After tonight, perhaps she should talk to one of the other guys.

He laughed. "I'm going to Kalamazoo myself...on business."

"Really?" She raised her eyebrows in surprise.

"Wanna ride along, keep me company?"

She frowned. "Together? Alone?" After her ruckus with Carl, she didn't want to be at the mercy of any man.

Snappy black eyes looked out from his sun-toughened face, a teasing smirk taking control of his expression. "No. Not alone. Rick is going with me. We're going to stay with friends."

"Oh." Her face flushed with humiliation and anger at her suspicious thought. "I thought..."

"I know what you thought. You were wrong," he said quietly, throwing her an understanding grin. "I'm not Carl."

"I'm sorry." She rose and stepped toward the door. "I think I should be going."

"You haven't answered my question. You have that habit, you know?"

"What habit?"

"Of walking out and not answering me."

"About what?" She turned to face him.

"About riding down to Kalamazoo with me."

She shook her head. "I don't think it's such a good idea."

He raised his eyebrows, a twinkle of mischievous deviltry flashing in his eyes. "What could it hurt? Rick needs a woman's influence once in a while."

"He's had his mother."

"Right, and pigs fly. Be serious. Will you come along?"

"I'll think about it." Again she reached the door and pushed it open.

"Haven't you forgotten something else?" His voice stopped her.

"What now?" She turned to face him again, agitation edging her tone.

"You don't have a car, or were you planning to walk back to Petoskey?"

"Oh." She shrugged her shoulders in resignation. "I must be completely addled tonight."

"Think nothing of it. After what you've been through it's understandable."

His words were warm, comforting and inviting. Oh, how she wanted to melt into the safety of his arms. For the first time in eleven years she needed someone. No, she needed Raul. She took a deep breath, squared her shoulders, shoved the weak thoughts aside and said, "Please, take me home."

He smiled, reached out and squeezed her hand in reassurance. "Everything will be okay," he promised.

She nodded, too choked by weak emotion to say anything. Paloma hoped he was right. Together they stepped into the cool night air that seemed to give her strength to regain her composure.

"Think about going downstate with Rick and me. You need the company." Raul opened the passenger door of the truck, helping her up the big step.

She stared into his eyes that reflected the moon. They seemed to caress her with gentle caring as they had so long ago. The desire to fall into his arms, to have him hold her close and gentle, was strong.

The problem was, every ounce of sense in her body told her the situation was dangerous, volatile, but she just knew she needed to be with him for a while. "I'll think about it," she said carefully.

Paloma wasn't sure she felt much better the next morning. She woke to a strangely quiet house. Inez had convinced her grandfather to go to the Upper Peninsula for a couple of weeks, much to Paloma's relief. Now she could decide how to handle the problem of finding her daughter without her grandparents being suspicious of her activities.

She sat up, her long hair falling over her shoulders in waves. She pushed it back from her tight, tear-stained face. Pulling herself from the softness of the bed, she rushed to the bathroom to splash cold water on her puffy eyes.

She stared into the mirror at her reflection. Squaring her shoulders she drew in a deep breath. "No more crying for you. You're going to find your child, make sure she's all right and then get on with the rest of your life." The white terry robe hung on the bathroom door. She grabbed it, slipped it on, and tied it at her waist on her way to the kitchen.

Paloma poured herself a cup of coffee from the pot she had programmed the night before. She took the plate of sliced melon and strawberries from the refrigerator and moved to the kitchen deck that overlooked Little Traverse Bay. Fog obscured the view of Harbor Springs across the usually blue-green water.

Sipping her coffee, she was drawn by the pull of the past when she and Raul had shared so many hopes and dreams. She closed her eyes, trying to catch a glimpse of the bliss they once shared. His return had filled her with bittersweet memories and it felt as if no time had passed since they had been in each other's arms.

"Stop this!" she reprimanded herself. It was important that she keep her mind on the difficult time ahead. She had no illusions that searching for her child would be easy. If she allowed disturbing thoughts of Raul to dominate her, she might never accomplish the task.

"This is crazy," she said, cradling her head in her trembling hands.

"Do you always talk to yourself?" Paloma spun around and saw Raul leaning against the turned support post. He was casually dressed in a cream color, cable knit sweater, dark brown, corduroy jeans and had traded his heavy work boots for a comfortable pair of Reeboks.

"I was just thinking out loud." She rose and stepped to the kitchen door. "Let me get you a cup of coffee."

"Thank you." He lowered himself to the chair of the redwood picnic set.

"What brings you around here so early?" She handed him the steaming cup.

"I came to have a word with your grandfather."

"Really? What about?"

"I wanted to ask his permission to take you to Kalamazoo with me." He reached across the table and took a large piece of melon, popping the whole piece into his mouth.

"You wanted to ask my grandfather? Don't you think I'm a little old for you to be asking my grandfather's permission for anything?" Her tinkling laugh filtered through the quiet morning.

He shrugged. "I don't know. I think he still thinks of you as his little girl. And he gives me the impression of being a bit old-fashioned." He glanced around. "Where is he anyway?"

"Gone to the Upper Peninsula. Gram and I thought he needed a little rest. He was getting too involved in the Timberland project and that's not good for his heart." She bit into a luscious red strawberry the size of a small plum.

"I'm glad for him. Maybe I'll take a little vacation as soon as this project is finished." He leaned back, stretching his long, muscular legs in front of him.

"A vacation does sound good." She reached for another piece of fruit, trying to keep her eye from the sensuous picture he made.

She looked up and saw him looking at her in a way she hadn't been looked at in a long, long time. Self-consciously she glanced down and saw the front of her robe had come apart just enough to expose the soft, generous swell of her breasts. Quickly, she gathered the folds of material and pulled them tightly around her.

He cleared his throat, a mocking smile turning the corner of his mouth. "Is this all you're having for breakfast?"

"It's a good breakfast, why?" Her gaze dropped to the fruit.

"I not only stopped by to speak to your grandfather, but I wanted to invite you to have breakfast with Rick and me. He's anxious to see you again."

"Where is he?" Her gaze breezed past him.

"Waiting in the truck."

"Oh, for heaven's sake. Why didn't you bring him in?"

"Because no one answered the door and I came around the house to see if your Blazer was still here, then I saw you on the porch."

"Well, let me get dressed and I'll come with you." Her face pink from embarrassment, she rushed into the house, then on second thought poked her head around the door and said, "Only because Rick wants to see me."

"Right," he called after her.

After Paloma hurriedly dressed and was about to emerge from the kitchen, Rick came around the side of the house.

"Hey, Dad. What's taking you so long? I'm starved."

"Paloma wasn't ready, so we have to wait for her to get dressed."

"Okay." The boy jumped over the railing. He crossed to the table and plucked a red strawberry into his mouth. "I hope Paloma doesn't mind."

"She doesn't mind." Paloma came out of the house, tying her braid at the end with a colorful elastic band.

"Hey, that was fast!" Raul said. His gaze swept over her tight jeans and heavy sweat shirt with the Michigan State symbol.

"Hi Paloma. Dad says you're gonna have breakfast with us."

"Dad says you want to have breakfast with me, and I find a handsome young man like yourself hard to refuse," Paloma teased in return.

It was cute to watch him color from embarrassment. He was a sweet boy, much like Raul must have been at his age. She placed an arm around him. "Come on, let's see where your father takes us for breakfast."

They all climbed into the truck with Paloma in the middle. Raul decided to take them to a small cafe downtown where the food was known for its home cooking quality.

"Are you going to come with us?" Rick asked, polishing off his lumberjack stack of pancakes.

"Come where?" Paloma asked.

"Dad says you're going to Kalamazoo too, so you might as well ride with us."

Paloma turned her gaze to Raul, and said, "I'm going to Kalamazoo, yes, but I'm flying."

"Aw, gee." Rick lowered his head in disappointment.

Paloma frowned at Raul. He didn't need to tell the boy she was going. There was no need to disappoint him. "I have my tickets already. I leave tomorrow at eleven."

"Can't you cancel them?" Rick appealed to her.

"I'm sorry, sport. I can't. But I'll tell you what I will do. When we all get back, I'll cook up some fried chicken and we'll all go on a picnic. Maybe down by the lake. How does that sound? It should be warmer by then."

"Not as good as going to Kalamazoo, but I love fried chicken." His boyish grin spread from ear to ear.

"Great." She reached out and ruffled his wavy, short cut hair. "You've never tasted chicken as good as mine."

"We'll keep you to that promise." Raul finished his coffee. "And who knows. Maybe we'll bump into you in Kalamazoo."

She yearned to take back her words and tell Raul she would go downstate with him. But it was utter madness to invite certain trouble. If she were to keep her child a secret, then she couldn't go with Raul. No matter how much she wanted to be with him and Rick, she had to go by herself. This was her secret to tell or keep, and caution told her to keep it. At least for now.

Chapter Five

"What do you mean, you can't find out?" Paloma leaned forward on the highly polished desk in the plush office of Lawyer Davis. "You arranged the adoption. If anyone can find out about my daughter, you can."

"Let me make this clear, Miss Ortega." The small, wiry lawyer who looked like some withered up old doctor from a '50s Western movie settled back in his chair and folded his hands across his chest. "When you signed the papers of adoption, you relinquished all ties to the child."

"Look. I'm going to find out about my daughter with or without your help, Mr. Davis. Coming to you was easier. But I can always get in touch with one of those organizations that fights to open the adoption records. What's the number...eight hundred, something search?"

"You don't want to do that. Why upset the present family? Besides, you'll have to wait until she's eighteen to contact her."

Paloma struggled with the uncertainty he had aroused. But he didn't seem to understand she only wanted to know about the child. "Look. I didn't come to claim my rights as her mother. I know I gave her up. But I have this deep need to know she's all right. That she's happy and loved. Can't you understand that?" She thrust her clenched fist into her chest.

The strain of fighting the situation was bringing her to the point of caving in. "I don't want to meet her or talk to her, or disrupt her family life in any way. I just have to know she's all right. I can be content with that." Her voice cracked.

His frown deepened as he rubbed his chin. He wore wire glasses perched on the tip of his nose and a Western style suit Paloma could tell was costly. And she'd bet the world that behind his desk, he had on a pair of expensive, leather cowboy boots.

"I'll tell you what I will do." He leaned forward, folding his hands on the desk. "I'll make some discreet inquiries about the family that adopted your little girl."

"Wonderful." She breathed a sigh of relief, elation flowing through her.

He held up his hand. "Now, don't get your hopes all blown out of proportion. I'm just going to find out how she is, that's all. They won't even know you've inquired about her."

"That's all I ask. Thank you very much." She stood and held her hand across the desk.

He shook her hand. "Give me a few days." He picked up the pen beside the blue scratch pad. "Give me the phone number of your hotel and I'll call you when I find out anything."

"Thank you, Mr. Davis. You don't know how much this means to me."

The door to his office suddenly burst open. "Hey, Davis, I got finished a little early and..." Raul stopped dead in his tracks and stared at Paloma.

Paloma's heart almost stopped beating. What in the world was he doing here? Had he somehow found out about their child? Then it hit her square in the fact. Raul had used Mr. Davis to set up his business years ago. That's how she knew he was a good lawyer, the only lawyer she knew when she needed one.

His eyebrows shot up in surprise as he glanced from Paloma to the lawyer. "Paloma? What are you doing here?"

Mr. Davis rose from his chair and glanced at the old schoolhouse clock hanging on the wall. "Raul, my boy. We weren't supposed to meet until lunch, remember?"

"I know," Raul answered slowly, his gaze fixed upon Paloma. "Your secretary wasn't at her desk and I came right on in. I'm sorry."

Paloma grabbed her jacket from the back of the chair, her hands trembling. "I must be going." Her throat tightened as their gazes met and locked.

"Paloma? Is anything wrong? Are you in trouble? Is that why you came to Kalamazoo?" Raul reached out and placed a gentle questioning hand on her arm.

"Raul." Her voice was soft like the spring breeze that played through the trees outside, though her thoughts were racing a mile a minute. She had to say something.

Taking a deep breath, she said, "Mr. Davis is helping me with some personal business."

The lawyer cleared his throat. "I see you know each other." He watched the interchange between the two, perplexity written across his expression.

Paloma jumped in before Raul could answer. "Mr. Fernandez is the general contractor on the job where I've contracted the mechanics."

She bit her lower lip. Inside she was a mass of quivering jelly, her nerves ready to make her a babbling fool. "I really must be going." She stepped toward the open door and past the flustered secretary. "Call me when everything is ready, Mr. Davis." She fought to keep her voice unwavering.

Raul moved in. "Listen. Since we all seem to know each other, how about lunch?"

"Together?" Paloma asked, feeling even more the idiot. Of course together. What else would he have meant? Bumping into Raul at the lawyer's office was one turn of events she hadn't planned on. *Dios,* what a fool she had been to use the same lawyer Raul had.

She pulled the sweetest, most innocent smile she could muster and said, "I really have a lot of business to take care of, so perhaps I'll see you later." She rushed from the room.

"Where are you staying, Paloma?" Raul's voice followed her, but she reached the open elevator and disappeared inside just as the doors slid shut.

Shaking, she left the office building. This was the most difficult time she'd been through yet. Then guilt slipped around her like a shrouding fog. Didn't he have a right to know about the child? After all, he hadn't purposely abandoned them. He never knew he was going to be a father.

What a mess. She had to keep her mind distracted from worrying over Raul and the turbulent times ahead. First and foremost was her daughter. Finding out about her was all important. Then came Raul. Logic told her he had every right to know about his daughter, but she had to keep rigid control over her emotions.

Once she found out about her child, then she could deal with Raul's rights. That was cold, she knew, but that was the way it had to be for now. But no matter how long she put off telling him, she was going to have to deal with it sooner or later.

She took a cab to her hotel and changed into comfortable walking shoes. A long walk through old familiar places might clear her muddled brain, help her think more clearly. Being here brought all the feelings that she kept under lock and key flooding back. The first time she'd met Raul was right here in Kalamazoo. She'd been seventeen, full of life and bursting free of childhood and starting her first year in college.

Her modified hiking boots made a clicking noise on the concrete as they took her from one street to the next. Suddenly she realized she was not far from the college.

Not far from the neighborhood where Raul and she shared that wonderful little apartment.

All the streets were lined with maples and elm, just as she'd remembered. It was as if time had reversed itself and she was back in college. Outside the tall brick house, she stood gazing at the windows on the third floor.

"Raul." She said his name aloud without realizing it.

"Pardon me, miss?" an elderly woman said as she passed Paloma. "Were you speaking to me?"

Paloma pulled herself from her dream-state. "No. I was just thinking aloud." She gave the woman an apologetic smile.

Had it really been twelve years since she and Raul shared that little apartment behind those lace-covered windows? It was as if she were only on her way home to meet him after class. To wait for him to come through the raised paneled front door of their small living room.

Raul, big, tall, extremely handsome and full of zest for life and laughter. Raul who would pick her up and swing her around when he came home and kiss her until she felt the world disappear around them; Raul whom she fell in love with at first sight.

She remembered feeling so special because he'd singled her out to be his girl. Although she had been young, she knew Raul was for her. She knew she would love him throughout eternity. And she'd been right. Raul...

Shaking the thoughts from her mind, she moved on down the street. The little corner grocery where she ran to get milk and bread was still there; still the little mom and pop operation it had always been. Tears threatened but she blinked them away.

Unable to stop herself, she traveled around the neighborhood, drinking in all the old haunts that only two lovers would know. Then she found herself standing outside The Little Brown Jug Cafe. This was where Raul asked her to be his wife, to share the rest of his life with him. Where she had said yes.

Squaring her shoulders, she pushed on the glass door. The familiar little sleigh bells tinkled as she went inside. She was greeted by the warm, delicious smells of hamburgers and French fries and music from the juke box.

"May I help you, miss?" A young waitress in a pink uniform approached her with a menu.

"I'd like a coffee, please."

"Sure, this way." She led Paloma to a small table by the back window.

Why had she come here? Not to Kalamazoo, but to all the old places she and Raul had frequented? Nostalgia threatened to suffocate her. She should have stayed at the hotel and read a good book or something. This was becoming too painful.

"Mind if I join you?"

Paloma jerked up and found herself once again staring into the most beautiful brown eyes she'd ever seen. "Are you following me?"

Raul shook his head. "Maybe. May I join you?"

"No...I mean yes, please sit down." Careful. He might think you've lost your mind. But she'd been trying to stay away from him to get her thinking straight. It had been useless. Everywhere she turned, she ran into Raul. And when she wasn't with him, his vivid memory haunted her.

Raul looked at his watch. "It's almost dinner time. Aren't you hungry?" He looked at her half cup of coffee.

She glanced at her own watch. "Is it that time already?"

"You'd better take good care of yourself or you'll find yourself getting sick."

"I'm all right, really."

"I'm not so sure about that. Fruit for breakfast and coffee for dinner. What did you have for lunch?"

She stared blankly at him. Lunch? "I...I ah..."

"Just as I thought. You didn't have any, did you?"

She lowered her gaze. She'd been so taken up with memories she'd forgotten to eat. Well, stress did that to her. And there was certainly a lot of stress lately. "I was preoccupied."

"Not too preoccupied to eat. You're skinny as a rail now. "Waitress," he called across the room. "Bring us a menu, please."

Paloma shook her head. How dare he demand she eat? What right did he have to force food on her if she didn't want it. "No. Really. I'm fine. I'm not hungry."

"Nonsense. You've got to eat something. What's your special?" he asked the waitress who now stood with the order pad in her hand.

"Chicken basket. And the soup of the day is homemade vegetable."

"I'll have the chicken basket and a bacon cheeseburger. And for the lady, a grilled chicken sandwich, light mayo, a thin slice of tomato and a cup of your homemade vegetable soup." He handed the menu back to the girl.

Paloma was about to argue but thought better of it. Now she realized how hungry she really was, and her mouth watered thinking about the chicken sandwich. And her heart swelled. He'd remembered how she liked it, right down to the light mayo and tomato.

"Brings back old memories, doesn't it?" He glanced around the room that had changed little in the past twelve years. It still had the same long, oak counter with red vinyl bar stools and the old multi-colored juke box in the corner. Vivid memories flashed through her mind of them dancing to their favorite song.

"Memories?" she asked nervously. She didn't want Raul's mind dwelling on the past. Their past. Nor did she want any conversation about their time together. It was too painful. She leaned back as the waitress set the steaming bowl in front of her.

"Eat your soup." He smiled mischievously and handed her the soup spoon. "Remember how you loved the veggie soup here?"

Paloma took a taste. "Mmm. Delicious. It's the very same." She took another spoonful.

"See, you have to eat."

"I know, but I get my mind on business and I forget the time."

"Is this business anything I can help you with? Are you in trouble? Davis is a damn good lawyer, but maybe I can help too."

Paloma shook her head. What would he think if he knew why she went to Mr. Davis? Would he hate her for not telling him about their daughter?

"No," she answered, averting her eyes from his, in case he should see the truth in them. "This is personal. And I can handle it." Her heart was beating out of control thinking he might find out about their child before she was ready to tell him ...if she was ever ready to tell.

"Sorry." He leaned back as the waitress brought his basket and Paloma's burger. "I didn't mean to pry."

"Tell me about Rick," she asked. If she could get him to talking about his life, he'd leave hers alone.

His face brightened. "He's a great kid, he really is." He picked up a drumstick and took a generous bite.

"I think so too. So tell me about him. What does he like?"

"What all twelve-year-olds like. Sports, camping, swimming in the summer and snowmobiling in the winter, if we're lucky enough to be where the snow is."

"Do you travel a lot?" she asked, finishing her soup.

"The jobs usually take me to the South during the winter. This year I was lucky enough to come North and near friends at that." His wide brow furrowed. "Damn lucky too. I might never have found out Helena was leaving Rick alone so much."

"Do you think she might try to get him back sometime?"

His frown deepened. "She better not! Although I wouldn't put anything past her. I'll fight her all the way to the highest court if she tries. He's a great kid and never causes trouble, but left alone...well, who knows?"

She nodded. What about their daughter? Was she supervised by loving parents? Was she... Stop! she admonished herself. When the lawyer found out anything he'd call.

"How long did you have him before Helena went to court to gain custody?"

"Would you believe he was nine before she wanted him? But by then I'd built this construction business from the ground up and it was going great guns. She found out and must have decided that to get the boy was to get into my pocket. And she was right. I'd do anything for Rick."

"It must have been hard on him."

"Oh, it was. But I saw him every chance I could. He's with me now and it'll be over my dead body before anyone takes him from me again." His face pulled a frown. "I'm his dad in everything but blood."

Paloma reached across the table and placed her hand on his. "Of course you are." Guilt anew flowed through her. He was really a good father. What would he say if he knew he had a daughter...another child to make his family complete?

"Tell me about being a plumber. Isn't that a little unusual?" he asked and then took another bite out of the juicy piece of golden brown chicken.

She laughed. "As grandfather told you, I went on the job with him from the time I could toddle around. He taught me everything he knows about mechanics. Then when I graduated high school I thought I wanted to be a doctor. And then I decided to go to college and major in psychology."

"I remember. You wanted to open an office and help people with their problems." He smiled.

She flushed. "I did." She fought to keep from laughing. She'd thought her life was so perfect. She wanted to help others have the same happiness she'd achieved. That was before their breakup. Before the baby. Ironic how the values of youth can suddenly change and a person can see the world as it really is.

"But you became a plumber instead?" Raul broke in on her thoughts.

"When I came home from college, grandfather needed help in the office. I started there. Then I graduated to drawing up the jobs and then I began pricing and bidding them. Before I knew it, I was working side by side with

Pop and it seemed the most natural thing in the world. So, here I am... a master plumber and mechanical engineer."

"Do you ever regret not becoming a psychologist?"

She thought for a moment and shook her head. "No. People grow up and goals change. This is the real world and I like what I do."

"That's all that counts." He took out his wallet, tossed the tip on the table and handed the waitress money to pay for both meals.

Paloma reached into her purse for her wallet. "You don't have to pay for mine."

"I know. But I want to." He rose and helped her with her jacket, his hand touching the soft curve at the back of her neck. She knew she was in deep trouble when the sensation of his touch crept under her skin and caused her blood to race. His touch, his warm breath, the closeness of his muscular body all conspired to make her break her well-intentioned resolve to keep her emotions in check.

"How far is your hotel?"

"The other side of the university."

"Is it too far to walk?" Raul accepted his change from the waitress and held the door for Paloma.

"Not if you're in for a healthy walk. I'd say it's about ten, fifteen blocks."

"Game?"

Paloma cracked a smile. "Sure. Why not?"

The sun was bright in the west, casting an orange glow over the city. A warm breeze teased the tendrils framing Paloma's face. "I don't miss all the hub-bub a bit." She watched the cars zoom by at breakneck speed. No, she didn't miss the frantic pace of city life. Of course, Kalamazoo wasn't a large city compared to Detroit or Chicago, but for a girl who grew up in northern Michigan, it had always seemed large, overwhelming and exciting.

"I know what you mean." Raul strolled beside her. "I think it's the lifestyle here. It's a madhouse where drivers race through the city streets in a hurry to get nowhere. And the constant smell of exhaust fumes suffocates any hope of fresh air."

Paloma laughed and nodded in agreement. "I know. When I returned home after college it took me time to get used to the peace and quiet. Sometimes I'd wake up at night and listen to the deafening silence."

They crossed the street as the light turned red and even then had to hurry because of the turning traffic. "Like right now." Raul motioned to the car that honked to hurry them on. "Everyone is rushing home for dinner after a long day's work. I remember fighting the traffic." He smiled down at her. "I still fight it. Do you know how many big cities I've driven through these last ten years I've been in construction?"

"You traveled extensively? Did you take Rick with you?"

Raul nodded. "I took him everywhere with me. I had a fifth-wheel. It was our home."

"How did you send him to school when he was of age?"

"One of the guys on the crew is married to a teacher. I home schooled Rick and she was his teacher. It worked out well until I lost him. Helena put him in public school."

"What about now? What are you going to do about his schooling now?"

Raul was thoughtful for a moment. He shrugged. "I suppose I'll have to settle down and make a home for him. A real home."

Paloma's heart beat rapidly. Where would he settle? But what business was it of hers anyway?

"You know," he took a stick of peppermint gum and offered her one, "you've made me think. I have to contemplate what I'm going to do. Making a home for Rick is first priority. It kinda looks like my days on the road are numbered."

"No more home schooling?" she teased.

"I don't think so." He seemed to ignore her jest. "He likes little league and all the other sports activities public school offers. And he needs the companionship of boys his own age. I have to think of Rick first."

They came to a small park. "Let's go through here and you can tell me all about those big cities you've traveled through." Paloma turned to the small concrete walk through the sheltering maples.

"I've lost count." He reached down and pulled a long blade of grass the city mower had missed and placed it between his teeth.

"This is the first time you thought of settling down then?"

He gazed at her. "I liked life on the road, all except the lack of family. Now that I have Rick again, I have to make some changes. That's what I came to see Davis about. I'm going to get custody of Rick permanently and then no one can take him from me again."

She saw the pain flash through his eyes. He deeply cared for the boy, that was obvious.

Engrossed in talking to Raul, she failed to see the dark, spring storm approaching. When the thunder crashed and lightning slashed across the sky, she shivered. The sky opened and droplets of water dotted her jean jacket.

She pulled her jacket up around her neck and held it tight. "I guess we'd better get moving." She began running toward the large brick building in the next block. "I don't care to take my shower out here," she called over her shoulder.

They raced along the wet street like a couple of laughing school kids, their feet making slapping sounds on the cement. They fought to get inside the hotel through the revolving glass door together. Laughing, they stumbled into the empty, shadowed lobby.

"I'm soaked." She felt her hair plastered to her head. Another angry rumble of thunder reverberated, shaking the building. Lightning pierced the gathering dark of the afternoon as the once orange sky churned angrily.

"You're shaking." Raul pulled her into the warm circle of his arms. "You'd better go up to your room and take a hot shower."

"You're soaked too." She felt his wet sweater plastered to his skin. "Do you want to come up and dry off?"

He was looking at her that way again. The way he looked when he wanted to make love.

"That's a foolish question, princess. His eyes darkened to jet, desire and passion flashing through them. "But I don't think we'd better invite danger, not right now. If I come upstairs, I won't be leaving."

He leaned forward and lightly touched her lips with his. "The sparks are still there, love. I'd best go."

He was right. She could lie to herself all she wanted, but her body screamed the truth. Her entire body felt hot and shaky. "I think...ah...yes, I suppose."

He lowered his lips to hers again and whispered against them, "This is too soon for you. I don't want you being sorry you let me stay."

She was wavering in her resolve to keep Raul at arm's length. She wasn't handling things as well as she wanted and she had been only a hairbreadth from caving in and inviting him to her room.

Just when she felt she'd crumbled beneath his gentle seduction, he pulled away, his gaze a soft caress. "I'm going before it's too late." He gently brushed her lips with his and turned, disappearing into the pouring rain.

❦

Paloma didn't sleep well. She'd tossed and turned, reliving old memories of her days and nights with Raul in that little apartment. Nights spent wrapped in the safety of his strong arms. She couldn't sleep even though it was still dark outside.

It occurred to her as she sat in the middle of the king size bed, that she could admit for the first time in a very long time that she needed someone. When she first met Raul, she fell for him hook, line and sinker. She'd lost her heart so long ago and she was in great danger of losing it again.

She wanted a home and family. His home and his children. She wanted him. Was it too late to pick up the pieces and start over? There was still the fact they shared a daughter. Would he still be attracted to her when he found out she'd kept such a monumental secret?

The rain suddenly eased and the deluge reduced itself to a wind-driven drizzle that splattered gently against the window. She raised her fingers to her lips that still tingled from his kiss. She wrestled with the hot emotions the kiss had unleashed, trying in vain to control them.

It wasn't as if she'd never been kissed before. But no one had ever kissed her like Raul kissed her. No other kiss had made her feel the throbbing ache that pulsed through her. No other kiss could ever fill the empty place in her heart. Only Raul's kiss could do that.

"Oh, Raul." A tearful utterance slipped through her lips. She still felt desire for him and it was growing stronger every day. He was dominating her every thought. She wished she could put him out of her mind.

And then when sleep did come in the wee hours of the morning, her dreams were filled with Raul and their lovemaking. The dreams had been so real, she awoke with a start, perspiration dampening her forehead, desire for fulfillment raging deep within her.

Chapter Six

After that restless night, Paloma stepped into the shower, letting the hot water pelt her tired body, trying to wash Raul from her thoughts. But he stubbornly lingered around the edges of her being.

She had dried herself, wrapped herself in her terry robe and begun blow drying her hair when the phone rang.

"It's kind of early, don't you think?" she said into the receiver, expecting to hear Raul's voice.

"Miss Ortega?"

"Yes." She felt warmth creep into her face. She knew better than to answer the phone that way, but she hadn't been able to resist, positive it was Raul calling.

"This is Mr. Davis. I'd like to see you in my office this morning."

Paloma's heart almost burst through the wall of her chest. Surely he couldn't have learned about her daughter so soon. "Is it about my daughter?"

"I don't want to talk over the phone. Can you be in my office at nine?"

Paloma glanced at the travel clock beside her bed. Eight. That gave her an hour to get ready. "Of course. I'll be there." She replaced the receiver with a less-than-steady hand and stared at the phone. Dare she hope? What was he going to tell her? Why didn't he want to talk to her over the telephone? Had something happened to her child?

She took a deep breath. Get a steady grip, she admonished herself. Lawyers don't talk business over the phone. It is only good business procedure to meet in his office, she assured herself.

In the closet she looked through the limited items of clothing she'd brought with her. Finally selecting a soft green pair of pleated pants, a matching jacket and a brilliant white shell, she laid them on the bed.

This is crazy, she told herself. You're acting as if you're going to see your daughter instead of only learning about her.

❦

Paloma sat in the waiting room of Mr. Davis' office. She'd arrived at nine o'clock on the dot. It was now nine-twenty. She watched the minute hand of the clock on the wall as it ticked by so irritatingly slow. Five minutes, ten minutes, fifteen minutes, and still the office door remained closed.

She picked up a magazine and thumbed through it without seeing anything in it. But just turning the pages kept her occupied. Kept her mind off the slowly ticking clock that got louder and louder by the moment. She wanted to scream. What was taking him so long? He'd told her to be here at nine and she had been. Why did he keep her waiting like this? Hurry up and wait. That seemed to be her lot in life lately.

Finally, when she thought she couldn't stand the waiting any longer, the door opened. "Please, come in, Miss Ortega."

Paloma tossed the magazine on the table and followed him into his office, taking the seat opposite his desk.

He took a file from the shelf and opened it. He thumped his thumb on the desk as he scanned the papers before him. Looking up, he removed his glasses and pressed the bridge of his nose with his forefinger and thumb.

"Is anything wrong?" Paloma asked anxiously.

He glanced up, concern written on his face. "It's not good."

"Is she ill..." She crossed herself. "*Madre Santo*, please, don't let her be dead." Fear circled her like a vulture.

He shook his head. "It's not that bad. The adoptive mother died about a year ago. She and your daughter were close. She's had some trouble adjusting since her mother's death."

"And?" Paloma prodded.

"It seems she's giving her father a hard time. She stays out late at night and he doesn't know where she is. She's changed her friends and is running with an older, wild crowd. She's become sullen and rebellious and he doesn't know what to do."

"Oh, *Dios*," Paloma gasped. "She's just a baby, only eleven. How can she do these things?"

"I knew the family when I arranged the adoption. Not personally you understand, but through a mutual friend. Anyway, it was the mother who wanted to have a child, not the father, I understand now. He was content the way things were."

Paloma frowned. "You mean he never wanted her?"

"I can't say that. He loved his wife dearly and would do anything to make her happy. Your daughter made her happy."

"Oh, what a mess." Paloma groaned, envisioning a child who'd just lost her mother only to feel neglected by a father who never wanted her.

"That's not all," he continued. "She ran away from home about a week ago and hasn't returned. Her father has no idea where she is."

"Oh, dear God, no." Fear for the child she'd never known consumed her. The vision of a small dark-haired girl roaming the streets unsupervised, running with a fast crowd that could very well suck her into all kinds of terrible things, haunted her.

"Even if she turns up, I don't think the father wants her back."

"What?" Paloma exclaimed. "Not want her? Not want his own child?"

"That's just the point. He's never thought of her as his daughter. And now he's planning to remarry and the child's only in the way."

Paloma stiffened. "How could anyone be so heartless?"

Mr. Davis settled back in his chair. "Some people in this world are just not cut out to be parents. He's admitted as much. I have to credit him for that."

"Maybe you can, but I can't." Paloma rose and paced the room, her brain a whirl of thoughts. What was she going to do? How could she help. "I have to do something to find her," she muttered.

"You?" Mr. Davis said. "How could you begin to find a little girl you've not seen since birth?"

"Could you get me a picture?"

"I can get one, yes. But I don't see how that's going to do any good."

"Just get me that picture." A primitive plan was beginning to form in Paloma's mind. She turned to the lawyer. "She's been living in this city, right?"

He hesitated answering.

"Look. We both know that child is in trouble. And you know where she is, or where her family is. Wherever she is, I'm going to find her."

He slumped back nodding. "You have a point. She was adopted by a couple from right here in Kalamazoo, a Spanish couple, as you requested. I assume she's still in the city someplace."

"Get me the picture. I'll take it from there."

He nodded. "I'll call your hotel and let you know when I have it."

Paloma left his office and began roaming the streets. Every little girl of about eleven with dark hair, she scrutinized. Could that be her? Maybe this one is my daughter. It took all the strength she had not to approach some of the girls that seemed lost and alone and ask who they were.

After relaxing and gathering her thoughts at a small cafe down the street from her hotel, Paloma returned to her room. When she looked in the mirror, she didn't look any different than she had a month ago. But today she was a mother looking for her child. What had gone wrong? Mr. Davis promised her the baby had been placed with a loving couple who would give her everything she needed. Well, he'd forgotten about the most important thing. Love.

"Oh, God," she whispered, feeling the same fear she'd felt that fateful day she'd handed the baby to the nurse. She should have demanded to meet the couple that would be taking her child. She would have picked up on the husband's indifference. Mothers had second sight concerning their children. "*Madre Santo*, please let my baby be all right."

Just a kid herself when the baby had been born, her first mistake had been to give the baby up. She should have faced her grandparents' disappointment and kept her daughter. They would have adjusted after a time. She should have found a way of finishing college and keeping the baby too. Lots of young women kept their babies today.

Tears welled up in her eyes. No sense in thinking about what ifs. She couldn't change the past. She had to concentrate on the present, on finding her daughter and putting things straight. With the back of her hand, she brushed the escaping tears.

The shrill ring of the phone pulled her from her thoughts.

"Hello?"

"Miss Ortega, your daughter's adoptive father has expressed a desire to meet and talk with you. Is it convenient to come to my office again this afternoon...say about two o'clock?"

"Of course. I'll be there."

She'd barely replaced the receiver when the phone rang again.

"Hi, Paloma? It's me. How about lunch?"

What a time for Raul to call. She couldn't talk to him right now. Her mind was too muddled with seeing her daughter's adoptive father. She couldn't trust herself. Not now. Not yet.

"I can't. I have business today."

"Then how about dinner? Rick has gone to camp with his friend for a couple of days and I'm sorta at loose ends."

Talk about loose ends. "I don't know..."

"Paloma? What's wrong? I can hear it in your voice."

Oh, *Madre Santo!* How she wanted to throw her burdens on him. To be gathered into the warmth of his arms and told everything was going to be all right. But that couldn't happen, not yet.

"Listen, Raul. I have personal things to take care of. Call me later. I'll see about dinner, okay?"

"Can I help?"

She heard the concern in his voice. But she couldn't chance telling him, not yet. "Give me a little time. Call me tonight, please?"

"Got a pencil?"

"Yes. Why?" she asked.

"I want to give you my hotel number. If you need me for anything, just call."

"All right." She wrote the number and address of his hotel on the pad beside the phone. "I'll call if I need anything."

"I mean it. Call me if you need anything."

"I will."

"Promise?"

"I promise."

"I mean it. I'm here for you if you need me."

"I know."

"Miss Ortega, this is Luke Mendoza." He and his wife adopted your daughter."

"How do you do?" Paloma said, a slight edge of bitterness spilling into her words. She scrutinized the tall man with thinning dark hair.

"Have a seat, please." Mr. Davis motioned to the chairs as he took his own.

"This must be very difficult for you," Mr. Mendoza began. "Believe me, this is more difficult for me."

I doubt it, Paloma said silently to herself. "What happened? Why did she run away?"

Mr. Mendoza shook his head. "Gabby...that's what we called Gabriella because she talked all the time. Anyway, she and I never got along." He held up his hand as Paloma leaned forward about to speak. "Hear me out before you get the wrong impression."

Paloma settled back. The least she could do was give him a chance to speak.

"I loved my wife dearly. She was the world to me, everything I ever wanted in a woman. She was sweet and gentle, kind and thoughtful. What she wanted most in the world was a child. We couldn't have our own, so she wanted to adopt. When we learned about your little girl, she wanted her more than anything. And she was a wonderful mother."

"What about you, Mr. Mendoza? Were you a wonderful father?" Paloma couldn't help saying.

He hung his head and swallowed hard. "I tried to be, I really did. I never wanted kids, you know? Not even our own. I was happy with just the two of us. But I admit, although I tried, I was a lousy father."

Silence hung heavy in the room for several seconds before Paloma murmured, "And my daughter paid the price."

Luke shrugged. "I don't blame you for being bitter. Things couldn't have turned out worse. I tried to help her after her mother died, but I didn't know how to ease her pain. I had my own pain."

I'm her mother! Paloma wanted to scream. "What about family...grandparents, aunts, uncles, or cousins? Where were they during all this?"

"That's another problem. Both our parents are dead and my only brother lives in California. They don't have any children either. My wife had no family to speak of."

Wonderful. Just what a child needed, a father who didn't want her.

Luke continued, "Then I met my new wife-to-be and things went from bad to worse. I still love my first wife, but she's gone and I have to go on without her. I'm going to get married again and Gabby won't accept it. She won't accept anything I do. She thinks everything I do is wrong."

"How long has she been gone?" Paloma asked, trying to keep the anger she felt in check.

"Five days ago she told me she was going to her friend Lori's house, but she didn't. That's the last I heard from her."

Paloma reached into her purse for a pad and pen. "Tell me this Lori's address and phone number." She jotted them down. "Did you bring me a picture?"

Luke reached into his jacket pocket and pulled out a small silver frame. "This was taken for her school picture this past winter.

With trembling hands Paloma reached out for the photo. She was going to see her daughter for the first time in eleven years. It was a three by five. A small, angelic child stared out from the photo. It was unusual for a school picture. The girl was sitting on a tree stump with her arms crossed over her knee. Her long, chestnut brown hair was drawn into a single French braid that hung over her shoulder, except for wild, frizzy tendrils that framed her face. And her sweet smile held the mischievous look of her father...of Raul.

Tears burned in her eyes but she blinked them back. Don't get emotional. Now isn't the time, she told herself.

"I have a suggestion," Mr. Mendoza said. "I think you'll go along with it."

"What?"

"I want to relinquish custody and give her back to you if you want her."

If she wanted her! That was the last thing Paloma expected to hear. She was being handed back her daughter as if she were damaged goods. As if the child hadn't been good enough.

What kind of a man was this? He acted as if children were disposable goods. If they cause a little trouble, throw them away. Get on with your life and forget them.

"No problem." She glared at him with burning, resentful eyes. "I will find her and when I do, I'm going to take her home with me."

Mr. Davis broke in suddenly. "You realize this situation must be handled with the utmost caution."

"You think I don't know that?" Paloma rose, clutching the picture to her chest. "But she's my daughter and I'll do anything to make her life right again."

"I hope you can." Luke rose and stepped to the door, relief visible on his long face. "I'll have her things packed. When you find her, she's yours."

"I'll draw up the papers for you to sign."

Paloma watched Luke incline his head and leave the office without a worry or care in the world.

"What kind of man is he?"

"I'm sorry." Mr. Davis straightened the papers in front of him. "These things happen. At least your daughter wasn't molested or abused."

"Thank God for a few favors. Now, where do we go from here?

Mr. Davis removed his glasses. "I'll have the papers drawn up and Mr. Mendoza will sign away his rights, giving you full custody of your daughter. But you have to find her first."

Paloma picked up her purse from beside her vacated chair. "I will, believe me."

"How are you going to go about it? I mean, I have this investigator friend of mine, I could..."

"No thanks." She stepped to the door. "I have an idea of my own. Just get those papers ready to sign. When I find Gabby, I'll be back."

❦

Now what? She asked herself as she walked the streets of Kalamazoo. This was becoming a habit, walking and looking at every little girl of about eleven. But now she had a picture. She pulled it from her purse and studied it. Gabby was a perfect mixture of Raul and herself.

Her hair a little darker than hers, she had Raul's eyes. Oh, they were brown like hers, but they were shaped like Raul's with those mysterious gold flecks. And she had his generous mouth and smile. Gabriella definitely had her nose and stubborn chin. She smiled. Was she as free-spirited as she herself had been at eleven? And did she have Raul's zest for life? She must, she ran away didn't she? She was making a definite statement.

It was almost five o'clock by the time she returned to her hotel room. Slumping on the bed, she thought and thought, making plans and changing them. There was only one solution she could come up with.

Raul. She held the slip of paper with his hotel and phone number between her fingers. Clutching it to her breast, she closed her eyes and wondered what his reaction would be. She rose from the bed and stared at the telephone. There was only one way to find out. Call him.

"Raul?"

"I wondered if you would call. Dinner?"

Paloma glanced around the room. It was large enough and certainly offered enough privacy.

"Yes, I was calling about dinner. Would you like to come to my room for dinner? I'm ordering in."

There was a silence at the other end.

"Raul? Are you still there?"

"Yes, ma'am, I am. You just surprised the hell out of me, that's all."

"We need to talk."

"Paloma?" The jesting in his voice faded. "What's wrong?"

She sighed and clutched the receiver tightly to her ear. "I can't talk over the phone. Please, come to dinner at eight and I'll explain everything then."

"Can't you give me a hint now?"

"Eight," she stated firmly.

"All right, eight it is."

She had three hours. That was enough time to order dinner and decide just how she was going to tell Raul about his daughter. She needed all the bolstering she could get. The hotel room suddenly became confining, stifling. She had to get out for a while. Grabbing her jacket, she rushed out the door for one of her habitual walks.

Down the street, a little boutique caught her eye. A lovely outfit in the window almost called to her. This was just what she needed to wear when she had her talk with Raul.

She gave herself one last glance of approval in the mirror. The blue outfit fit her like a glove. A little gold crucifix that her grandparents had given her years ago seemed to give her courage beyond her own, as if they were there with her, giving her strength. And the gold chain Raul had given her caressed her skin for the first time in eleven years.

"Okay," she whispered to the picture of her daughter. "Now, all we have to do is wait. Hold on, baby. Everything's going to be all right."

She'd pulled the table out to the balcony. It now boasted a white lace table cloth and two blue candles. The evening was warm and still, the weather having changed almost overnight. But then it didn't take a genius to remember that two hundred miles made a world of difference in temperature.

Her heart raced when someone knocked on the door. Raul. It had to be Raul.

"Come in." She held the door for him.

"Wow." He gave a low whistle "Don't you look beautiful tonight?"

"Thank you." She felt her cheeks burn under his scrutiny.

He reached out and ran a finger over the gold chain circling her neck. "Nice," he murmured, but the passion that flashed in his eyes told her he wasn't talking about her chain. "Am I wrong, or is that the one I gave you?"

"You remembered," she whispered.

"How could I forget?" When he removed his hand she could still feel the warm touch of his fingers against her skin. How intensely aware of him she was. This was foolish, she admonished herself. Now wasn't the time for passion. She had to tell him something that could very well crush any hope for a future together.

He removed the light jacket that covered his Henley shirt and placed it on the edge of the bed. The shirt was unbuttoned just enough to expose the massive chest she had known so well.

Before either could speak, another knock sounded at the door. "Please take it out to the balcony," she motioned to the delivery boy pushing the serving cart.

Raul lifted the lid and found a porterhouse steak, rare. "Looks good. Seems I'm not the only one who remembers." He winked.

After she'd tipped the boy and they were alone, she lit the two candles. "Let's sit down."

"Okay, Paloma. What's this all about? What's going on?"

Tears burned in her eyes. She couldn't bring herself to look at him. She had to tell him, yet it was the hardest thing in the world she'd ever had to do. What if he hated her when he found out? What if he refused to help her find their child? God forbid, what if he washed his hands of them both?

She placed her head in her hands and gulped back a sob.

Raul was around the table and kneeling before her, taking both her hands in his. "Paloma. Please, tell me."

She crossed herself and clutched the golden cross. "Oh, Raul. I've made such a mess of things. Of my life. Of our lives." The tears ran down her face. And she couldn't stop the sobs that ripped from her throat.

Raul pulled her up and into the warmth of his arms, holding her protectively close. "Whatever it is, it's going to be all right, I promise."

"But you don't know. You don't understand what I've done." She sobbed as if her heart would break.

"Whatever it is, we'll work it out together, I promise."

"You're going to hate me. I warn you, you'll hate me." She buried her face in his chest, tears soaking his shirt.

Raul tilted her chin up so he could gaze into her tear-filled eyes. "I could never hate you. Not in a million years."

"But you will when you find out," she wailed.

He laughed. "Find out what? Are you secretly the Hillsdale Strangler or something?"

A faint smile touched her lips. "If it were only that simple."

"Why don't you just tell me what's wrong and we'll go from there."

Paloma pushed herself from his arms and went to get the picture on the bedside stand. She picked it up, turned to Raul and handed it to him.

He looked at it and then at Paloma. "What are you trying to tell me. She yours?"

Paloma nodded.

Raul laughed again. "And you thought I'd hate you for having a child? How shallow do you think I am?"

"Look at her, Raul. Look at her long and hard."

He did. He studied the picture. "I see a delightful young image of the woman standing before me."

"Look again. Look hard. Can't you see it?"

Raul frowned as he studied the picture. "I just want to know where you've been keeping her?"

Tears spilled from Paloma's eyes again as she bit the back of her knuckles. "Don't you know? Can't you see by looking at her? Raul, she's eleven years old."

Raul looked at the picture again. Slowly he raised his gaze to hers, a frown deepening, drawing his eyebrows together. "Are you trying to tell me...? You don't mean she's...?"

"*Madre Santo!* I knew you'd hate me. Oh, Raul. I'm sorry. I hate myself." She sobbed again, only this time she wasn't in the security of Raul's arms.

"She's mine?"

Paloma couldn't speak. She just bit her lower lip and nodded.

"Mine? I have a daughter and you never told me? How could you keep something like this from me?"

Was that anger in his voice? Or was it hatred?

"I'm so sorry," she whispered, tears spilling down her face anew.

"I have a daughter?" He studied the picture of his daughter. "Where is she?" Emotions from perplexity to awe burned in his face.

Paloma shook her head. "I don't know."

"You don't know? What do you mean, you don't know?"

"This is so hard." The ferocity of his indignation was frightening. Her breaths came in rapid gasps, her breasts rising and falling in rhythm with her sobs. "It's a long story."

"I have all the time in the world, so how about starting at the beginning." His nostrils flared as he fought for control.

She took in a long breath, trying not to break down again. "Give me a minute." She turned her back. This was worse than she'd imagined. He hated her yet he wanted to know about their child. That was good.

Slowly she faced him, praying what courage she had left wouldn't desert her.

"She's run away."

"From you?"

"No, she doesn't know about me. Not yet."

Raul shook his head and held up his hands for her to stop. "Wait a minute. We have a daughter. You don't know where she is but she's run away. You don't know her and she doesn't know you. What kind of sick game is this?" His expression was bewildered and dazed as he fought to understand.

"Believe me, it's no game." She drew in another breath. "Just let me tell you my way."

Raul sat on the edge of the bed. "All right. I'm listening."

"Before we broke up, I suspected I was pregnant."

"And you left me because of that?"

"You said I could tell you in my own way."

"Okay, Okay. Go on." He held up his hand in a sign of acceptance of her conditions.

She couldn't look at the disappointment in his face. She stared out toward the balcony as she continued. "As I said, I thought I was pregnant. I was so happy until Helena came to the apartment to tell me you and she had gotten back together, that you were getting married, that the baby she carried was yours."

"I didn't know she was pregnant when I left her and she never told me until after you had gone out of my life.

You have no idea what life with Helena was like. I wasn't sure the baby was mine even after she told me."

"But you went back to her," she said quietly.

"You were gone and if the baby was mine, I had an obligation to it. I couldn't leave a child to the mercy of an unfit mother." He gave an impatient shrug. "But, what about you? Why didn't you tell me about our baby?"

She gasped for air. "You were going back to Helena, at least that's what she said. I couldn't keep the baby alone. My grandparents had such strict morals that if they knew we had been living together without marriage, it would have broken their hearts. To them, I was living in sin and to top it off, I got pregnant. I couldn't tell them that. And I was all alone."

She stopped to gather her thoughts and this time Raul remained patiently silent, not interrupting her.

"I told my grandparents that I had to take special classes so I could take the classes I wanted the next fall, and that I had to go to school all summer. I really stayed behind to have the baby. When I saw her, I wanted to keep her, I really did. She was so small and helpless, so sweet and beautiful, but I wanted to do right by her too. She deserved to have a family who'd love her and want her and give her everything I couldn't. So I gave her up for adoption."

Raul jumped up. "That's what you were doing at the lawyer's office yesterday. He helped you, didn't he?"

"Yes. He was the only lawyer I knew because I knew you used him."

"When did you decide to find her?"

"I've always wanted to. I was waiting until she was eighteen and then I was going to contact her. But you came back into my life and I knew I had to know she was all right. That she was loved and cared for, but I found out different." Again the tears fell.

"What do you mean? Have you found her?"

"I've found the adoptive family. The mother died about a year ago and the father doesn't want her. He never wanted her."

"Where is she then?" He gazed at the picture in his hands.

"She ran away from home. She's out there in this city somewhere. Alone and scared."

Shaking, Paloma went to the table that held the now cold dinner and poured herself a generous glass of wine to steady her nerves.

Without another word, Raul picked up the telephone and dialed a number. "Gomez, this is Raul. When you get in, call me. It's important. No, damn it, it's an emergency!" He left the hotel number on the recorder.

"Now, we're going to wait for Gomez to call." He sat on the edge of the bed.

"Who is Gomez?" Paloma asked in a small voice.

"He's a PI, a friend of mine. If anyone can help us find her, he can."

"Thank you."

Raul rose and paced the floor. Then he poured himself a glass of wine. "I can't believe you'd give up a child. Our child."

Paloma stiffened. "I didn't want to. I did it because it was best for the baby. I couldn't take care of her and finish college," she gasped. "I was just a kid myself, alone and unable to confide in the only people who could help me."

"You should have told me."

"I believed Helena. She seemed so sincere."

"But that was my child you carried. That was my responsibility too. I should have had a chance to say what I wanted." He shook his head. "I can't imagine giving my own flesh and blood away." His tone was accusatory.

Anger traveled through her body like a bolt of electricity. "Do you think I wanted to? Do you think a day goes by that I don't think and wonder about her? For eleven years I've worried about her, wondering where she is and how she's getting along."

"At least you knew about her. I never even knew I was a father."

A silence hung heavy between them.

Before either of them spoke again, the telephone rang.

Chapter Seven

They both stared at the ringing phone, then at each other. When Paloma didn't move, Raul reached across the bed and answered it. Relief relaxed the tense muscles along his jaw. "Gomez. Thank God, man. I need your help and fast."

Paloma sat on the edge of the bed shaking, listening to Raul tell the unseen person on the other end of the line about his daughter. This stranger was learning her secrets of the past. Could things get any worse?

"I'll see you in the morning then." He hung up. "He's leaving right now. He should be here in three and a half hours."

"Is he good?" Her head whirled with doubts. What had happened to the level-headed young woman she'd been yesterday?

Silence hung between them for several seconds before Raul spoke. "Good?" He cleared his throat. "Gomez, you mean? Yes, he's as good as they come and the best friend a guy could have."

"I hope so. If I have to open my private life to someone, they better be good."

Raul didn't seem to be listening. "I'm a father. I have a daughter." His face clouded in bewilderment.

Paloma rose and closed the space between them. She laid a gentle hand on his arm. "Just listen to yourself. You've been a father for a long time. You're Rick's father."

He lifted pained eyes to her, confusion playing around his mouth. This wasn't the Raul she knew. He had to snap out of it. She depended on him to be her strength. Someone she could lean on during the bad times.

"Of course, I'm Rick's father." His dark eyes showed the tortured dullness of disbelief and perplexity. He held up the photo of their daughter. "But this is my daughter. My flesh and blood and I never knew she existed."

Paloma reached out and turned his head toward her. "Does it really make any difference? Do you love Rick any less since you learned of Gabby?"

"Of course not."

"Then pull yourself together. We need each other. We both have to be strong. We're in this together." She regarded him with searching gravity.

He returned his gaze to the photograph.

"Stay with me here, Raul," she said, sounding more in control than she really was. "We have a daughter out there and even though she doesn't know it, she needs us. We have to be strong for her. She's going to need every bit of support we can give her."

"I know," he said. "But I've never felt so strange and confused in my life. I usually know what to do in any given situation. But right now I feel betrayed and angry. Can you understand that?"

Paloma gulped back a sob. "It's all my fault and I'm sorry. I can't take it back. I can't make it right. What I did, I did. But we can go forward and work together to salvage what's left." She reached out and took his hand in hers. "Let's concentrate on our daughter, not ourselves. We're not important, she is."

"This has been one hell of a shock. But you're right, she's the most important person in all this."

Paloma boldly moved closer. "Do you think you can learn to forgive me in time? Please, Raul. Don't hate me too much. I couldn't bear it."

"I don't hate you, Paloma. I just have to get used to this." He gently pulled his hand free. "I have to leave for a while. Do you understand? I have to be alone. To think."

She nodded. "Are you coming back?" she asked, wishing she could take the words back as soon as they left her mouth. There was fear in her tone. Whatever might have been between them was now over. Her confession had smashed a tender recapturing of their past. The condemning expression in his eyes told her that.

"I'll be back. I need time to think." He moved to the door, his back straight, his shoulders tight and his face grim.

She wanted to ask him to stay. She wanted to tell him she needed him. But with as much pride as she could muster, she watched him walk out of her room and probably out of her life forever.

❦

Hours later after walking the streets of Kalamazoo, Raul ended up on a park bench outside Paloma's hotel. Had he been so terrible that she feared to tell him she was carrying his child? No, it hadn't been anything he'd done, it had been Helena's lies that had caused the trouble. Damn! If only he had known, he would have made damn sure he hadn't lost Paloma. He would have explained that Helena must have gotten pregnant just before he left. Of course, he would have had to deal with Helena, but he would have had both of his children. And none of this mess would have ever happened.

Wearily, sometime before dawn he walked to his truck and headed for his hotel. Somewhere during his wanderings that night he came to the realization that Paloma had done the only thing she could. She'd been a tender eighteen and had a strong pride her heritage gave her; a pride that made her walk away when she thought he didn't want her any longer.

He began sifting through his tangled thoughts. As much as he resolved otherwise, as much as he shoved the thought from his mind, as strongly as he fought it, he had to admit he still loved Paloma. And honestly, he always had. It hadn't been just sexual. It still wasn't. He loved her. Her. With that acknowledgment came the realization that he had to tell her so. He couldn't lose her again.

The clock on the dash said six o'clock. Dias. Gomez must have gotten here hours ago, while he was out walking the streets feeling sorry for himself. After returning to his hotel room, he took a hurried shower, changed his clothes. and headed back to Paloma's hotel.

❦

Paloma had slept little during the night. At one o'clock in the morning Raul's friend Gomez had knocked on her door. After quick introductions, she told him Raul wasn't there, so he took a room for the night, saying he'd see them both in the morning.

This had been the most horrible night of her life. If she thought worrying about her daughter was stressful, combining it with Raul's disillusionment doubled it. She was like an egg teetering on the edge of a razor blade. One slip and her whole world could come crashing down.

How was she going to survive this? How would she stand his hatred? His disappointment? She remembered his angry face, his cold, distant voice, and it tore at her heart. She swallowed hard and faced the possibility that he might hate her for the rest of her life, even though he'd said he could never hate her.

Deep in her depressing thoughts she turned on the shower as hot as she could stand, letting the full blast of the prickling water wash over her, trying to wash away her troubles. Finally turning off the water, she reached for a towel, wrapped herself, and was about to step out when the bathroom door opened.

She jumped a foot. "You scared me to death! How did you get in here anyway?" she gasped.

Raul stood there, his gaze traveling over her scantily covered body. The smoldering flame she saw in his eyes startled her, yet warmed her heart. He wouldn't look at her like that if he hated her. Would he?

"The maid let me in. Amazing what a few dollars will do." His face suddenly lost its lightness and turned serious. "We're in this together and I think we have to get a few things straight."

Paloma nodded, clutching the towel tighter around her shivering body. "Okay. But let me get dressed first."

The smell of fresh coffee greeted her when she came out of the bathroom dressed in a pair of jeans and a green flannel shirt with a black turtle neck sweater under it.

"Here. Have a coffee." He handed her a cup. "First of all, I want to say you were right. We're in this together for good or bad. And we both made a lot of mistakes along the way that led us here. And I agree, what's behind us is behind us. We have to go on."

Relief flowed through her. At least he wasn't walking out and leaving her alone.

"Agreed?" he asked.

She nodded, too choked up to speak. He had no idea how much she wanted to hear him say those words. To know he was standing beside her in this terrible mess.

"I ordered breakfast. Do you want some?"

"Not fruit, I take it." She tried to put a little levity in her voice to keep herself from caving in to tears.

"Yes, I knew you'd want fruit, but there's all the rest as well." He dug into his plate of scrambled eggs and bacon.

She was just about to say she wasn't hungry when someone knocked on the door. She admitted Gomez.

"Gomez, this is Paloma, Paloma Ortega. Paloma, Gomez."

"Yes. We met in the wee hours of the morning," Gomez said, seating himself in one of the velvet chairs by the window. He took out his little notebook and reached over for a long, crisp piece of bacon.

"Have some breakfast?" Paloma offered.

"This is fine, but I will have some coffee, thanks." Gomez flipped through his notebook. "Let me get this straight." He read from the handwritten pages and repeated what Raul had told him the night before. "And you want me to find your daughter. What have you got for me besides the name and address of her adoptive father."

Paloma stepped to the bedside table and picked up Gabby's picture. "Her fath...adoptive father gave us this." She handed him the picture. "And I have the name of her best friend. I think you might get some information there."

"Good." Gomez took the picture and put it in his jacket pocket. "Mind if I keep this? I'll give it back in one piece, I promise."

Paloma nodded. She rummaged around in her purse until she found the scrap of paper with the name of Gabby's friend.

"How about the police? Were they ever notified that an eleven-year-old child had run away?" Gomez asked.

Paloma and Raul glanced at each other.

"I don't know. Her father didn't say." Paloma shook her head.

"Well, never mind. I'll find out. I'm going to see the father first and then I'll go to the friend's. She's only eleven. If she's in the city she will have contacted her friends. At least that's been my experience in cases like this." He closed and stuffed the notebook in his pocket.

"I can't thank you enough," Raul said, holding out his hand.

"Let me find her before you start thanking me." Gomez finished his cup of coffee and stepped toward the door.

"We're going to stay in Kalamazoo, at least until you've found her." Raul threw a questioning glance to Paloma.

She nodded in agreement. Of course. Where else would she go? Wild horses couldn't drag her away until they found Gabby.

"Good. When I learn anything, I'll contact you." He opened the door and then turned back. "By the way, where are you staying in case I need you?" he asked Raul.

"I'll be moving here...I mean, getting a room here. It will be more convenient if we all are under the same roof."

"Right." Gomez held up his thumb. "I'll be in touch."

Paloma felt awkward being alone with Raul. "What are we going to do after we've found her, have you thought of that?"

Raul slowly shook his head, concern etched in his face. "Somehow we have to take her home. If her father doesn't want her, as you say, then it's up to us to make a life for her."

Relief flashed through her. "I was hoping you'd say that. That was my exact thought."

"The question is, how is she going to take finding out about us? I mean, she's liable to resent us. In her mind we abandoned her."

"I've thought about that. If I were in her place, I'd resent us too. So I was thinking, what if we act as foster parents for a while, until she learns to trust us. You know, bond with her as friends first, gain her confidence.

She watched doubt cloud his eyes. "Maybe. But she's sure to resent us when she does finds out. Wouldn't you, if the roles were reversed?"

"I suppose I might. But if we work to gain her respect and confidence and build a bond with her, then in time we will tell her who we really are. She's too fragile right now to know the truth. She would never trust us."

He poured another coffee from the insulated server. "I just thought of another idea."

"What?"

He shook his head. "I'll tell you later."

Paloma settled in her chair. It wasn't the most comfortable of chairs in spite of its expensive looks.

"We can't hang around here just waiting. We'll both go crazy." Raul rose from the foot of the bed. "Let's go somewhere."

"Where?"

He shrugged. "I don't know. Anywhere. Let's just go and see where we end up."

They left the hotel shortly after ten, driving away in Raul's pickup with the windows rolled down and the radio tuned in to a country-western station.

"Let's check in every so often in case your friend has found out anything," Paloma said above the sound of the music.

Nodding in agreement, Raul drove through town and to the outskirts. "Remember this?" He pulled into the park where they used to picnic those long years ago.

He gave her a quick glance. "Remember?"

"Yes." Her heart racing, she tightened her lips and looked down at her hands clasped tightly in her lap. She didn't want him to read his effect on her or what being here meant to her.

"Let's go see if it is still there." He opened his door and jumped out.

Paloma followed, knowing what he wanted to look for. "I'm finding it so hard to get past Gabby. I seem to be rooted."

"Me, too." He held his hand out to her. "But we can't sit around and wait. Gomez will find her. And when he does, we'll begin working for a future."

"I can't think of anything else."

"I know. But let's try." He pulled her across the new green grass of spring.

By a secluded body of water stood a grove of weeping willows. Swans gracefully glided along the sparkling water. The gentle, warm breeze whistling through the trees and the songs of several birds made it a day perfect for young love.

Raul held her hand as they made their way under the sheltering foliage of the swaying willows. "There it is." He pointed to a large heart dug into the trunk of the largest tree.

Paloma smiled, remembering the day Raul had taken his jackknife and carved their initials. It had been the day they decided to move in together, the most exciting, happiest day of her life. "After all these years," she mused.

"It's amazing, isn't it. I figured some kids would have carved our initials away or replaced them their own. Maybe it's a sign?" He studied her.

Paloma began to tremble. Surely she was reading the wrong meaning into his simple statement. He couldn't mean...

He turned her to him and looked deeply into her eyes. "We've both made a lot of mistakes. And we're paying for them now. But we have the chance to make it right, to recapture what we lost." He reached out and lightly ran his finger down her cheek to her lips and to the pulsating throb in her throat.

Paloma shivered, desire raging along her veins. Everything in her screamed for fulfillment, but a little voice nagged at the back of her mind that he was only doing this because of their daughter. She allowed herself to be pulled into the tender warmth of his arms.

"It's been a long time. Too long," he whispered tenderly.

Where was her strength? This shouldn't happen now. Not while that private eye friend of his was out combing the city for their daughter. But, heaven forbid, it felt so good, so right to be in his arms again.

The kiss deepened. It was the kiss she'd waited twelve years for. It was magic, as if they'd never parted. Only Raul could make her feel like this, make her weak with a single kiss.

"Raul..."

"You feel and smell so good, so sweet..." He pulled her closer, burying his face in her hair.

"Raul," she said through a fog-filled brain. "We can't, not here." She stopped his hands from going farther. If they didn't stop now, she'd be lost.

Raul glanced at her from passion-dazed eyes. "Why not? We did before."

She laughed. "I know. But we were kids then. What if someone comes along. Some kid?"

"That never stopped you before," he teased.

"Yes, but I was a kid myself then. We're responsible adults now. I don't think it would look too good for our pictures to be on the front page of the paper reading, 'Couple arrested for indecent sex acts in the city park.'"

He gave her a quick kiss. "You're right. Besides, I think I'm too old to try youthful acrobatics on the hard ground anyway."

She watched the barely suppressed flicker of desire sparkle in his eyes and the old, familiar smile she loved spread across his face. "Does this mean the spell is broken?"

A whimsical gleam danced in his eyes. He took her hand and led her back to the truck. "Nope." He opened the door and motioned for her to slide in. Then he slid in under the steering wheel and started the motor.

"Raul, what are you doing?"

He just smiled, said nothing and stared straight ahead. Then he stopped at a phone booth outside the park and still without a word made a call. When he returned he said, "No word from Gomez yet," and pulled away from the curb, heading outside of town.

Suddenly she knew where they were going. She felt her face burn red.

He glanced at her. "You remember, don't you."

She nodded. How could she ever forget? This was the very motel where they had first made love.

"Wait right here. I'll be back." He climbed from the truck and disappeared through the glass door that had the word Office painted on it.

The years rolled away. She felt eighteen again, remembering so clearly the night she gave him the one gift a woman can give a man only once. Her virginity.

He climbed back into the cab of the truck and dangled the key at her. "Room 22."

The same room. She couldn't believe it.

The room had changed over the years, but this was their special place. They'd come here more than once before they got their apartment together. Had stayed all night, not just had a quickie and left. They'd been in love. Really in love.

Was this going to be the sealing of a commitment, the rebirth of lost hopes and dreams? She wanted to surrender to him more completely than ever before, more deeply than before. She wanted to become his, totally and forever.

She had no chance to speak. His mouth covered hers with a kiss so consuming that she melted against him. Yes, yes, yes. This was how it was supposed to be. A deep, all-consuming hunger that burned through them both, yoking them in a world of their own, just the two of them in this self-made universe.

Slowly, boldly, she began unbuttoning his shirt, revealing his muscular chest, sprinkled with black, curly hair. She slipped it from his shoulders, all the while staring into his eyes. Then he did the same; unbuttoned the flannel shirt and slipped the black turtleneck over her head. Soon, there was a pile of discarded clothes on the floor. Gently, he lifted her into his arms and tenderly laid her on the bed and joined her.

His breath came faster as he covered her face with kisses, working his way down to the pulsating hollow of her throat. "Sweet, sweet Paloma," he groaned against her breasts. He was like a man who, dying of thirst in a vast desert, stumbled upon a cool, refreshing pool in a paradisiacal oasis.

Closing her eyes, she indulged in placing light kisses along his strong jaw and down his neck. She blew soft puffs of air in his ear and delighted in his sudden intake of breath. She thrilled in the feeling of power she had over his response.

His dark eyes darkened more with desire while his arms circled her slender body. "Paloma. Beautiful Paloma." His voice was barely a whisper.

"Kiss me again," she begged. "Kiss me." She felt dizzy as the fires of his passion consumed her. She wanted to burn, to feel his fire consuming her until there was nothing left but exhausted fulfillment. She needed to yield to the burning sweetness that was held captive within her.

Their bodies danced in rhythm to nature's oldest tune, creating their own kind of primitive music. Then a sound, partly a moan, partly a cry, escaped his throat, matched by Paloma's own primeval response as they soared together.

In the still of the afternoon they lay wrapped in each other's arms until the dance of love consumed them once more. Then they slept, spent and fulfilled. It was a couple of hours before either of them heard the slightest of sounds.

"Oh, my goodness. Look at the time." Paloma glanced at her watch. "Raul! Wake up!" She pushed against his shoulder.

He groaned like a man near death. "What? What's the matter?" He roused himself to one elbow, his eyes dazed and puzzled.

"It's almost five in the afternoon."

"We have to find out if Gomez has learned anything." Raul reached for the phone and dialed the hotel number, spoke as if he were talking to a machine and left a telephone number. He turned to her and shook his head as he replaced the receiver. "We're just too anxious. Gomez will find her. It's only been a few hours since he's been on the case." He rose from the bed.

Paloma pulled the sheet around her naked body, moved across the room and took a bath towel from the pile left on the vanity.

Raul's voice stopped her. "Are you going to take a shower without me? Remember when we...?"

She felt a flush stain her face. Did she remember? How could she ever forget?

"Do you really want to take a shower with me?"

"Would I have asked if I didn't?"

She nodded toward the bathroom. "Come on then." She dropped the sheet on the floor and disappeared through the door.

Hot water and steam filled the small room.

"I've missed this." Raul stepped beside her, took the soap and began rubbing circles over her back and down toward her buttocks.

She closed her eyes and savored the delicious feelings he was arousing in her once more. "If you keep this up, we may not get out of here very soon," she warned.

"So, what's wrong with that?"

She took the soap and began lathering his body. "Nothing, just that we should get back and wait for Gomez's call."

"Gomez has this number. We really don't have to hurry." They were wet from head to toe, but that didn't matter. Raul picked her up and moved again to the bed, and to the tune of the same primitive music as before, they rode waves of desire until they fell silent, satisfied and exhausted.

By his even breathing, Paloma could tell Raul had fallen asleep again She slipped from the bed, dressed and after running a comb through her tangled tresses, stepped outside to enjoy the day. Though the sun was still quite high, it had taken on an orangish afternoon glow. A warm breeze feathered her hair and played over her skin. Somewhere in the distance a bird gave a strange, forlorn call.

Raul moved behind her and placed his hands on her shoulders burying his head in the waves of hair cascading down her back. "You're finally awake." She reached up and placed her hand atop his.

"I suppose we should go," he whispered into her hair.

A soft moan slipped from her lips. She knew they should, but when they left, would they lose what they'd gained? Would all the murmured promises be lost?

Despite all the intervening years and all the distrust, she found herself wanting him more than ever. Wanting to keep what they had just rediscovered.

Hand in hand they walked back to the truck. With one last glance at paradise, she climbed into the truck beside him.

"You look as if you've lost your best friend," he said.

She kept her hands busy by smoothing her hair, pulling it into her neat, sensible French braid. Glancing out the window, afraid to look at him, she said, "You have to understand that I'm not that silly, impressionable teenager any more. I'm a woman. A responsible, well-respected woman who has worked hard to get where I am. This wasn't just a moment's fling. At least not for me."

"Did I give you the impression it was?" His voice became anxious.

"Dammit," she exclaimed in frustration. "You of all people should know how I feel. This whole thing has managed to turn both our relatively stable lives upside down. Neither of us knows what's going to happen next or how it's going to affect us."

"We can make a pact not to let anything affect us adversely, no matter what comes at us. We've found one another again. If we're determined, nothing can change that."

Warmth flowed through her. "You mean that?"

"Would I have said it if I didn't?"

No. He wouldn't. If Raul was anything, he was honest. He meant it right now, right this minute, but what if something happened with Gabby that would change it all later? Stop it, she admonished herself. You're just asking for trouble.

❦

Back at the hotel, Gomez reported and asked them to meet him in the hotel restaurant at seven-thirty.

Paloma changed into her green pants and white shell for dinner. Instead of pulling her hair back in a French braid, she brushed it to a sheen, pulled the sides back and clasped it with a pearl clasp, letting it wave down her back.

"What did you find out?" Raul held a chair for Paloma at the table where Gomez waited for them.

"I talked to her father. Nice guy." He wrinkled his nose and pulled a negative face. "And that little friend of hers."

"And?" Paloma leaned anxiously closer, her hands clasped under her chin.

"She's not talking, yet. I've talked to her parents and they're going to see if they can get something out of her. I could tell by talking to her that she knows where Gabby is. But she's a stubborn little thing for a kid, I can tell you."

Raul leaned back in his chair. "Do you think you'll find her?"

Gomez nodded. "Oh, I'll find her all right."

"You think she's all right?" Paloma asked. All she wanted right now was to know Gabby was all right. That she wasn't hurt or hungry or... She closed her eyes tight, afraid to think.

Raul reached over and placed his hand atop hers. "It's going to be all right. Gomez is going to find her. And when he does, we'll go from there."

Paloma heaved a deep sigh. "I know. But this is so nerve-wracking. I'm so strung out I could fly."

"Take heart," Gomez said gently. "I should have her within the next twenty-four hours."

"Really?" Paloma perked up.

"Really." Gomez picked up a menu. "Let's order. I've put in a stressful day and I could eat a horse."

Chapter Eight

"Phone call for Gomez Vaga," The waiter politely interrupted their conversation.

"Excuse me." Gomez rose, placed his napkin beside his plate and followed the waiter through the crowded restaurant.

"Wonder what that's about?" Paloma said, anxiously hoping it had something to do with her daughter.

"Maybe about Gabby," Raul answered, his voice mirroring her anxiety.

"I hope."

Gomez returned, wearing a disturbed expression. "They've found your daughter."

"Where." Hysterical excitement welled up in Paloma.

Gomez awkwardly cleared his throat. "She's in juvenile detention."

"She's where?" Paloma rose from her chair, but Raul put his hand on her arm and shook his head as several people at close tables turned and looked at her. "Be calm. Getting upset won't help anything."

"What is she doing there?" Raul asked.

Gomez cleared his throat again and glanced hesitantly at both of them. "She was picked up with a group of older girls—shoplifting."

"*Madre Santo!*" Paloma crossed herself and folded her hands together as if in prayer.

"Can we get her out?" Raul asked.

Gomez shook his head. "Not tonight. She'll have to appear before the juvenile judge in the morning."

"Oh, this is all my fault." Tears of grief burned in Paloma's eyes. "I never should have let her go. If I'd have kept her this would never have happened." She gulped back a sob.

"Don't blame yourself. We have to be strong and work together to get through this; to get her through this. Remember what you told me earlier," Raul gently reminded her.

Paloma wiped her tears away with the back of her hand.

"Let's order some dinner."

"I couldn't eat." Paloma shook her head. *Dios,* who could eat at a time like this? Her nerves were raw and ragged. She had to get up and walk around...something. She couldn't just sit there and do nothing. If she appealed to the police...

Raul reached out and stopped her when she rose to leave. "You have to eat. You have to keep up your strength. She's going to need your strength when she gets out."

"I can't just sit here. I have to do something. There must be a way to get her out." Her expression appealed to Raul and then Gomez.

Gomez shook his head. "Not tonight. Only her legal guardian can do that, and he says let her cool her heels in the hall."

"Oh, how heartless," Paloma cried.

"You have to get hold of yourself, sweetheart," Raul whispered. "You won't do any good going off the deep end. Besides, who would give her to us just because we said we were her real parents? In the eyes of the law, we're not."

Paloma slumped back. It was hopeless. Her baby was going to spend a night in jail—juvenile hall—same thing. "She's just a baby," she whispered.

"It's not as bad as it seems." Gomez said. "She will have to appear before a judge. Being so young, that will probably be tomorrow or the next day at the most. Her adoptive father will most likely be there to relinquish his parental rights. The best thing the both of you can do is to be there."

"What good will that do?" Paloma asked.

"First thing in the morning, I'll get together with Davis and have him petition the court for temporary custody on your behalf."

She sighed in relief. "Do you think we'll get her?" Her eyes brightened

Gomez was eating his steak but spoke up, "With her adoptive father's consent, I see no problem. She's young. The court will look upon this as a chance to rehabilitate her. This will save them from putting her into a foster home."

Paloma watched the strange glances between Gomez and Raul.

"What?" She glanced from one to the other.

"Tell her." Gomez nudged Raul.

Raul shook his head. "It's not the right time. Not here."

Paloma was getting more than a little irritated with the interchange that was obviously involving her but leaving her quite in the dark. "What is this all about? What are you two scheming?"

Raul frowned. "I wasn't going to ask you until later." He glanced around the impersonal, unromantic hotel lobby.

"Ask me what? What are you talking about?"

"Gomez and I were talking and then I phoned Davis, who thinks it's an excellent idea."

She felt screams of frustration in the back of her throat. "Will somebody tell me what's going on before I lose my mind? What are you talking about?"

Raul took a deep breath. "If we were married, we'd be sure to gain custody of Gabby."

Paloma sat back, stunned. Married? Like this, out of the blue? No romance, no engagement, no nothing? "Married? This is what you meant earlier when you said you had something else in mind."

Raul leaned forward. "It's only reasonable. The courts like the foster home to have two parents. And since...I mean we..." He was suddenly at a loss for words.

Oh, she knew what he meant. They'd already been together intimately. They might as well get married. Under both Gomez and Raul's scrutiny she became increasingly uneasy. She looked away hastily and twisted her hands in her lap. This wasn't the way she had pictured his proposal, should there ever be one.

This was cold reality. This mess was partly her making, that was a certainty. Raul wanted to marry her. To make a family with their children. *Dios,* she'd forgotten about Rick.

"What about Rick? What will he think?"

Raul shook his head. "Don't worry about Rick. He likes you already. He won't mind. In fact, I'll tell him when I see him tonight."

"I suppose," she whispered.

"Is that a yes?"

"Yes." She forced a tight smile. "But we have to get a license and whatever else...how?"

Amusement flickered in the eyes that met hers. "All taken care of. I only needed your yes. We can be married in the judge's chambers in the morning."

"Judge's chambers? All taken care of? What judge?"

"Davis arranged everything. All you have to do is say I do, tomorrow."

Things were going too fast. Her head was spinning. It was like being on a non-stop merry-go-round. She wanted to stop the world and get off, if only for a few sanity gathering moments.

❦

Paloma thought the night before had been hard. It was a cakewalk compared to what she went through after dinner. She tossed and turned and when she did sleep, she had nightmares of the authorities dragging her daughter off to jail.

Without much sleep and sporting dark shadows under her eyes, Paloma got up and showered. Today, she, Raul and Gomez would be in court. But first they had a little visit to make to the judge's chamber.

After putting on her new blue pants suit, she applied just enough makeup to cover the dark circles under her eyes, a little lipstick and a floral scent. Then she pulled her mane of chestnut hair into a business-like French twist.

Standing in front of the mirror, she assessed herself judiciously. What was the use? She wasn't going to a regular wedding. This was out of necessity. Her grandfather and Inez wouldn't be there. They wouldn't even know about it until later. She squeezed her eyes tight. *Abuelo, what will you think when you find out? Will you be so very disappointed in me?*

She sat on the edge of the bed and held her head in her hands. What a mess. Whatever happened to her adolescent dreams? Dreams of wearing white and walking down the aisle on her grandfather's arm. A special honeymoon in the Canadian wilderness in a rugged cabin on a private lake, where she would spend hours in Raul's arms making passionate love.

Oh, what was the use of thinking like this? Destiny had stepped in a long time ago. It had drawn them to this very moment. Everything else was just fanciful dreams.

"Ready?" Raul poked his head in the door.

"As ready as I'll ever be, I guess." She rose and picked up her purse.

The judge's chamber was dark paneling, which cast shadows of depression over the already austere room.

A rotund man in a long black robe entered the back door. "I want you to know I am the judge who will preside over the juvenile case of your...your daughter." He picked up a folder and leafed through it.

Relief flowed through Paloma. If he was willing to marry them, then there was a very good chance he'd give Gabby's guardianship to them.

"I've gone over your request and your daughter's file. This little girl is in need of a lot of help. I feel that her real parents are the ones to give that help." He peered at them over the half-glasses perched on his nose. "Don't disappoint me. It's seldom I have a case I feel as good about as I do this one."

"Thank you," Paloma whispered in a small, respectful voice.

"Now." The judge picked up another book. "Stand together." He pushed a button on his intercom. "Miss March, will you come in here for a moment."

The small, dark-haired secretary bustled in.

"You will serve as witness at this wedding." He motioned for her to stand beside Paloma, while Gomez and Mr. Davis stood beside Raul.

The judge began to read the words that would bind Paloma and Raul together. Paloma felt nothing but a strange numbness, a disbelief that any of it was real. She repeated the words after the judge like some unthinking robot. Even when Raul took her left hand and slipped the shiny, wide gold wedding band on her finger, it didn't seem real. She stared at it as if in a foggy dream.

"By the authority invested in me by the State of Michigan, I pronounce you husband and wife."

That was it! They were married. Husband and wife, yet she didn't feel married. She felt...there were no words to describe how she felt. Empty?

The judge snapped his little book closed and handed them a pen to sign the license. Raul took the pen and signed, then handed the pen to her.

"The best to both of you in your endeavor. This little girl is going to need it." The judge seated himself behind his desk. "Now, I want to go over a few things with you before court. At your request, she will think she's being placed in a foster home. I agree with your decision. She's too fragile at this point to learn her true parentage. But I suggest you tell her when she's ready to hear it."

Paloma nodded. "We intend to."

"Good. Now I have to get to court. Mr. Davis will bring you in when your case comes up. It will be one of the last because this will be a closed session."

"Thank you." Raul held out his hand and the judge took it.

Alone in the judge's chambers, Raul reached over and placed a warm hand on Paloma's. "We should have done this a long time ago."

Paloma was still numb. "If we had, none of this would have happened to our daughter. We would have raised her in a loving home." She moved to the window and looked out at the moving traffic on the street blow, tears gathering in her eyes.

"You sound angry."

With her back still to him she said, "I am angry. Angry that this ever happened. Angry that I gave my baby away. Angry that I didn't tell you I was pregnant." The stress of the last few days came crashing down and she gave way to the tears she hated so much."

"Paloma, please. Don't cry." He tried to gather her into his arms.

She jerked away. She didn't want him to touch her right now. She needed to be alone to gather her thoughts. Of course this wasn't fair to him; she realized that. But it wasn't fair to her either.

"Raul, please. I need time."

Raul nodded. "I understand." He backed away.

But did he? Did he really understand that it wasn't him, it was the whole situation? Their lives had been changed in a matter of a few days. They would never be the same, their lives would never be the same. Would she ever again be that sensible, stable young woman she'd been before she began looking for her daughter?

Though the situation was strained, Paloma and Raul stayed in the judge's chambers for hours. Slowly, Paloma felt the need to talk and broke the ice by asking Raul's forgiveness for her resentment. But before Raul could answer, Mr. Davis came in. "You can come into court now."

They followed him into the closed courtroom. Sitting at the table with her adoptive father, her arms folded across her chest, was Gabby.

Paloma studied the young girl who had grown from the tiny, helpless baby she'd given birth to.

Her straight, dark hair was braided with black leather, matching her leather-studded vest. In her nose was a gold ring matching the one in her brow. She didn't look eleven.

She could pass for fourteen or fifteen with her eyes made up and her lips that ugly, deep purple.

"Stay calm." Raul whispered in her ear. "She needs us now more than ever."

Paloma reached out and took his hand in hers. He squeezed it, silently telling her he was with her. She could lean on him.

Gabby turned around and stared at them. The look wasn't hatred, it was a vacant look of abandonment, as if nothing mattered.

"Mr. Mendoza, it has come to the attention of this court that you are unable to control your daughter."

"Yes, sir," Luke Mendoza said with a nod. "She won't listen to a thing I say."

"Is this true, young lady?"

Gabby stared straight ahead without answering.

The judge sighed, his face reflecting his annoyance. "Then I have no other option but to place Gabriella Mendoza into a foster home of the court's choosing."

Paloma watched Gabby. She had no expression at all. She just sat there like a stone statue.

"In view of all the circumstances I have been given by Mr. Mendoza and Mr. and Mrs. Fernandez, I am going to make my decision short and to the point. It is the order of this court that Gabriella Mendoza will be placed under the foster care of Mr. and Mrs. Raul Fernandez, effective immediately." He closed the file.

The adoptive father stood and quietly walked from the courtroom. He looked straight ahead, not looking at either Raul or Paloma. He was a free man.

Forgetting him, Paloma concentrated on what she could do for that precious child. Underneath all that costume of rebellion was a sweet, angelic child and Paloma would find her and bring her home.

"Before you leave," the judge said, "my clerk has some papers for the two of you to sign." The judge motioned them toward his chambers. "And as for you, Miss Mendoza, you will be returned to juvenile hall until such time Mr. and Mrs. Fernandez come for you."

Paloma wanted to protest and as if Raul knew what she was thinking, he took her arm and led her to the judge's chambers. "Don't make a scene," he whispered. "We'll be back for her soon. We have to pick up Rick, collect our things and come back for Gabby."

"I'm really going to have a sister! Oh, wow!"

"Yes, I told you last night about her."

"I know," Rick said, "but I couldn't believe it."

Raul and Paloma shrugged their shoulders and glanced at each other.

"Listen, pal. Gabby has had a very hard life for the past year. She lost her mother and her father..." He glanced at Paloma for support. "Well, her father didn't want her anymore."

"Why?"

"He wasn't her real father. They adopted her and when her adoptive mother died, her adoptive father just didn't want to be a father anymore."

"What a geek."

Raul patted his shoulder. "Well said."

"Are we all going to live together?" Rick looked from Paloma to Raul and back to Paloma again.

Raul nodded. "We're a family now. And we're going to make Gabby a part of it. Do you think you can do that even though at first she's going to be...ah, a little trouble."

"Hah. A girl give me trouble? I don't think so."

"Remember, son. She's had a bad time. She's going to need a little time to get used to us and our life." He laughed. "We're all going to need a little time to get used to living together. This is a big change. Do you think you're up to it?"

Rick squared his shoulders. "Sure. What's to get used to? I've always wanted a whole family, now I got one."

Raul squeezed his shoulder. "That's my boy."

Rick put his arm around Paloma. "I'm so glad you're part of our family too. Remember when I asked you to come to Kalamazoo with us?"

Paloma nodded. "Yes, I do."

"So, you are going to ride home with us now, right?"

Paloma smiled to the point of almost laughing. "I suppose I'll have to, now won't I."

Rick picked up his duffle bags and headed toward the truck. "This is great, just great!"

All the way back home, Gabby remained silent, staring sullenly out the window of Raul's double-cab pickup. No matter how much Rick tried to get her into a conversation, she ignored him as if he wasn't there. She just sat there staring and snapping her gum. Finally, Rick gave up and was as silent as Gabby.

Early in the evening, they pulled into Paloma's drive. The large Victorian looked lifeless. Only the orange glow from the sunset reflected in the windows facing the bay made a welcoming gesture.

"Well, here we are." Raul opened the door and stretched from the long ride. "I'll help you inside with your things." He and Rick began unloading Paloma and Gabby's things.

"I think it best if you stay here the night and begin moving into my place tomorrow. What do you think?" Raul whispered so only Paloma could hear.

"Good idea. I hadn't thought about where we'd live."

"Together is a good guess since we're married." He threw her a wicked grin.

Of course, he was right. Where else would they live? Apart? That would defeat their whole plan to help Gabby. Yes, tomorrow they would begin moving. Right after she checked in on the job.

The job! She'd forgotten all about it. Only a short time ago, the job had been all-important. Things had sure changed in the last few days. Would she ever get back on track?

"Come in, Gabby. I'll show you to the room you'll use tonight." Paloma followed Raul into the foyer and dropped the cases beside the staircase.

Gabby slowly moved in behind them, looking at her new surroundings.

"Listen, kiddo," Raul patted Gabby on the shoulder, "Rick and I have to be going but you and Paloma will be moving into our new house tomorrow."

Gabby's pulled a frown. "I want to go home!"

"This is your home now, dear." Paloma put her arm around the girl's shoulder.

Gabby jerked away as if burned, her face reflecting fear and uncertainty. "This will never be my home. I want to go back to Kalamazoo."

"Please try." Paloma kept her voice deceptively calm. "We're all tired, but after a night's rest..."

Gabby backed away and said quietly, "I hate you. I hate all of you." She moved toward the door. "You can't make me stay here. You can't force me to do anything I don't want to. And I won't stay, I won't." Tears gathered in her liquid brown eyes as she fought against revealing any emotion. She whirled toward the door only to run right into Rick.

"Hey, watch it. You coulda run me over."

"Get outta my way. I'm leaving."

"Oh, yeah? Do you want to wind up in jail again? Besides, where ya gonna go? Huh? Have you thought of that? Don't be stupid."

His cold, pointed words stopped her in her tracks.

Paloma moved toward her. "Gabby, I know this is hard for you. But Rick is right. Staying here is much better than spending another night in jail." She put her arm on her daughter's shoulder. "Let me show you your room."

Sullenly, with rebellion written across her face, Gabby bent to pick up her duffle bag and followed Paloma up the stairs.

Raul winked at Paloma when their gazes met. "I'll check on you in the morning."

"I'll have breakfast ready for all of us before I begin packing. Seven?"

"We'll be here." Raul and Rick disappeared into the twilight of evening.

Paloma led Gabby along the hardwood hall to the guest room. "I think you'll be comfortable here." She flicked on the light, sending a warm glow over the yellow and white room.

"I hate yellow." Gabby slumped on the bed.

"What colors do you like?" Paloma asked, removing the decorator pillows from the bed.

"What difference does it make?"

"It doesn't. I was just remembering that when I was about your age, I was getting pretty sick of everyone pushing pink off on me."

"I don't like pink either, so don't get any stupid ideas. Pink is for sissies!"

Oh, this was going to be something, dealing with a rebellious, unhappy child with a chip the size of the world on her shoulder. Paloma took a deep breath. "I wouldn't think of it. So, what do you like? Green? Red? Blue, maybe?"

"Black."

Of course, what else had she expected from a kid trying to act tough.

"Would you like a black bedroom?"

Gabby showed emotion for the first time. Showed surprise. "You'd let me have a black room if I wanted it?"

Okay. Keep it cool. Now is not the time to butt heads with this little spitfire. "If you want black, then black it is."

"You're kidding, right?"

Paloma shook her head. "I don't kid about serious stuff like bedroom colors." She removed the yellow, flowered comforter, folded it and placed it in the window seat.

"All right, then I want a black bedroom. Everything in black."

Paloma shrugged her shoulders. "Okay, we'll go shopping tomorrow after we've looked at your room at the other house."

"What other house?"

"Raul's house. He has a beautiful new log home. That's where we're going to move."

"Whose house is this?" Gabby glanced around.

"This is my grandfather's house. I grew up here after my parents died."

"You lost your parents?" Gabby's face reflected surprise.

"Yes, but I was much younger than you."

"And your grandfather still wanted you? Even after your parents were gone?"

"Yes. Both my grandparents wanted me."

"Oh."

"May I ask you something, Gabby?"

"Sure."

"Did it hurt to have your nose pierced?"

Gabby reached up and felt her ring. "No, silly. No more than it did to have my ears done. Why?"

Paloma shrugged. "I don't know. I just wondered. Besides, I never knew anyone who had body parts pierced."

"It's awesome. You oughta try it."

Paloma shook her head and held up her hands. "No thanks. I'll stick to my ears."

"Chicken."

"Yes." Paloma laughed and nodded. "I guess I am. Now tell me. What do you like for breakfast?"

"Hey, are you trying to win me over? 'Cause if you are, forget it! I don't get won over very easy."

Dios, what a smart kid. "You could say that. Or you could say that I'm just being extra nice on your first day here. So? What is your favorite breakfast?"

"Pheasant under glass."

Paloma fought from cracking a smile. So this was how it was going to go. Oh, well. "Fresh out. What's second." She lifted the window just a crack for fresh air and adjusted the blinds behind the lace curtains.

"Oh, waffles and sausages, I suppose."

"Waffles it is."

"With strawberries and whipped cream?"

Oh, she was good. Real good. "With strawberries and whipped cream. But I have to warn you. The strawberries are frozen. No fresh ones until later this summer."

"That's okay."

"Hey, I'll tell you what. How about you take a bath or shower, whatever you like, and I'll change into my night clothes and pop some popcorn and we'll watch a movie I have. How would you like that?"

"Popcorn and cheese?"

Paloma nodded. "Popcorn and cheese."

Paloma dialed Raul's number from her bedroom. "At least I've got her talking."

"Good. It's a start."

Paloma yawned. Bed. She wanted more than anything to crawl into her bed and sleep, but she couldn't. "I promised Gabby popcorn and cheese."

"Sounds good. Maybe Rick and I should come over."

"Maybe."

"No. I think you should try to crack that shell she's built around herself."

"You're right. I just wanted to tell you she's talking."

"Okay. See you in the morning, love."

"Night, Raul."

After her shower, Paloma pulled on the pajamas she hadn't worn for a couple of years. Next came the fuzzy robe and slippers. Now she'd check and see how Gabby was doing.

She knocked on her door. No answer. She knocked again. Maybe she was in the tub or shower. She turned the knob and poked her head in and called, "Gabby. Are you ready for popcorn?"

Still no answer. Paloma stepped into the room. Gabby was nowhere. The bathroom door stood open and empty.

Paloma's heart flew into her throat. Where was she? Had she run away again? Oh, no.

Paloma raced through the upstairs looking in every room. No Gabby. Downstairs was the same. Why would she run away in a strange place? Rick had been right. There was no place to go.

"Gabby," she called as she yanked the doors open to the patio.

"Yeah?" Gabby's voice filtered in from the dark.

"There you are." Paloma forced herself to calm down and breathe easy. "I was wondering if you were ready for popcorn yet?"

"What's that?"

"What?" Paloma's gaze followed where Gabby's finger pointed.

"Those lights across the water? What is it?"

"That's Harbor Springs. It's a little town across the bay. Some call it Petoskey's sister town."

"It's pretty."

Paloma leaned on the railing beside Gabby. "Yes, it is. The water is called Little Traverse Bay. It empties into Lake Michigan."

"Why do they call it little Traverse Bay?"

"Well, because the larger Bay near Traverse City is called Grand Traverse.

"You said you grew up here."

"I did."

"Do you like it here? Really like it here?"

"I guess so. I've never lived any place else, so I don't know for sure. But I would like to go to Mexico again. I have family who live there. It's nice and warm all year."

"I want to travel and see the whole world someday."

"You will if you really want to."

"Ya think?"

"You can do anything you set your mind to. I'm a master plumbing and mechanical engineer. And when I started it was the beginning for women to go into any field they wanted."

"You're kidding, right?"

"Nope. I'm a plumber."

"Radical! Go for it, girl!"

Paloma fought to keep a straight face. It would take time for Gabby to leave her punk talk behind, but they had all the time in the world. "I'll take you to work with me tomorrow and you can see for yourself what I do."

"Really? You'd take me to work with you?"

"Sure. I'd love to have you with me?"

"Bitchin'. My dad said I was just in the way. He wouldn't take me to his work."

Damn the cold-hearted beast. He had made this child the way she was. Well, if she had anything to do with it, she'd help her develop into a responsible person who believed in herself. "You might even be able to help me."

"My dad didn't like me, you know. That's why I'm here. I heard him say once girls were worthless."

Tears hid behind that hardened expression. Paloma's heart broke in two. What a burden for a little girl to carry. If she could get her hands on him, she'd wring his neck!

"You know, Gabby, you're here because you got into trouble. But some people are just not cut out to be parents. Kids scare them. Your father was like that."

Gabby looked up into Paloma's face, moonlight reflecting in her eyes. "Scared? Why would anyone be scared of a kid?"

"Not really scared of the child, but scared of the responsibility of being a parent. Kids have to have rules and grownups have to set examples for them. Some adults just can't do that, so kids scare them to death."

"Do you think that's why my dad didn't like me?"

"It wasn't that he didn't like you. He was a very frightened man. He is scared to death of children."

"That's stupid." Gabby shook her head. "A grownup being scared...of a kid! But they adopted me." Her face grew sad and serious. "My mom told me I was special. She said she picked me out of all the other babies."

"See, you were special. Your mother told you so and you should believe her. And your father, well, he doesn't know what a special girl he had. That's his loss. It happens, kiddo. She reached out and put a careful arm around her daughter. "Now, how about that popcorn and movie?"

"Is it a good movie?"

Paloma led her inside. "I think you'll like it. It's about a Mexican-American girl named Selena. She was a singer who worked hard to make it to the top of the charts. She makes our people proud. It shows if you work hard, you can do or be anything you like."

"I remember Selena. I had some of her CDs."

"Let's make that popcorn and watch the movie."

After the popcorn was popped, Gabby curled up on the sofa with a big bowl in her lap. Paloma pushed the tape into the VCR.

"Why don't you live with Raul?"

Paloma jerked around. "What?"

"You're here and he's...someplace else."

Paloma laughed nervously. "That's simple enough. Raul and I just got married this weekend."

Gabby's face reflected surprise. "You did?"

"Yes, yesterday to be exact."

"Rick isn't your son?"

"No, he's Raul's son by his first marriage." She sat down beside Gabby. "It's a long story and I'll tell you all about it one day. But for now, I'll just say that Raul and I have known each other since college. We met again and fell in love. We married while in Kalamazoo and we will move into his house tomorrow."

"Oh." Was all Gabby said as the movie came on. Obviously that short explanation had been enough to satisfy her curiosity.

Chapter Nine

"Come in," Paloma called through the screen door. "Breakfast is just about ready." She took a square, golden waffle from the iron griddle, adding it to an already tall stack.

"Something sure smells good in here." Raul entered the kitchen followed by Rick.

They both glanced around. "Where is she?"

"Still sleeping." Paloma put the waffles in the warming oven above the antique stove.

"You could go wake her." Paloma nodded to Rick.

"Not on your life!" He backed away, waving his hands. "I like living, man."

"You'll find her a little more mellow this morning. Just be careful what you say." Paloma took the strawberries and whipped cream from the refrigerator, placing them in the middle of the round table. "Tell her the waffles are done. She's in the room to the left at the top of the stairs."

Rick was hesitant, but he went in through the dining room.

"Just be sure you knock first and wait for her to answer. No lady likes to be barged in upon." Paloma threw him a warning smile.

"Rough night?" Raul plucked his fingers into the strawberries and took one that wasn't quite mashed.

"Those are for breakfast." Paloma swatted his hand.

"Blissful, married life. I can see it already." He rolled his eyes heavenward.

"Oh, stop being so melodramatic." She put everything on the table. "Coffee?"

"Please. I'm about to have a caffeine fit." He seated himself next to the patio door. "So, how did last night go?"

"Not bad, actually. Although I thought she'd run away again."

"Why? What happened?" He jerked a glance her way.

"I went to her room. We were going to watch a movie and have popcorn. Anyway, she wasn't there. I searched the house and she was nowhere." Her eyes widened when she relived her fear. "You can imagine the scare I had. I found her outside just staring across the bay."

"At least she's still here. That's an accomplishment."

"I'm taking her to work with me today." Paloma poured more coffee in her cup.

"Do you think that's a good idea?"

She glanced across the table at him. "And what are you going to do with Rick today?"

"Touché. I have to take him with me too. Well, I don't have to, but he wants to go."

Paloma sat at the table, holding her cup between her hands. "She opened up to me just a wee bit last night. She wanted to know why her father didn't like her."

"Oh, God. What a thing for a child to carry. I could kill that guy for what he's done."

"I know how you feel. I told her how some people just weren't made to be good parents and that children scared them. I told her, her father was that kind of person and it had nothing to do with her."

"And? How'd she take it?"

Paloma shrugged. "She seemed to take it well enough. I told her how my parents died when I was small. That seemed to give us a familiar ground to build on."

"Maybe we can get Dad to take us horseback riding or to Mackinac Island or maybe both." Rick and Gabby rushed into the kitchen.

Paloma vowed not to comment on Gabby's black clothing, nor the makeup she'd plastered on her face that gave her that punk look that was really out of style.

"Breakfast is served." Paloma rose and took the waffles from the warming oven.

"That's a funny looking stove." Gabby studied the gray and white 1935 porcelain stove with the rounded warming ovens across the top.

Paloma laughed. "That's my grandmother's pride and joy. She never had such luxury in Mexico, I can tell you. When it went kaput, Grandfather had it rebuilt."

Gabby helped herself to the waffles, pouring strawberries and topping them generously with the spray can of whipped cream.

"Where are they now? Your grandparents?" Gabby asked with a mouth full.

Ignoring the fact that she wanted to say she should not speak with her mouth full, Paloma said, "On a little vacation in the Upper Peninsula. Have you ever been up there?"

Gabby shook her head, her mouth still full of breakfast.

"We'll all go for a weekend before the summer is out. Is that all right?" she asked Raul.

"Sure. Maybe we'll even go before your grandfather gets home so we can all spend time up there. You said he had a cabin up there?"

"By a lake. Really, it's only a small lake. We own it. It's wonderful for swimming and the fishing is great."

"Fishing. I can't wait!" Rick exclaimed, dicing earnestly into the breakfast.

"I've never been fishing," Gabby said shyly.

"You'll love it," Rick said. "That is, if you don't scare the fish away with that get-up of yours."

Gabby frowned, glancing down at her attire.

"Rick," Raul admonished, "apologize to Gabby."

"Aw, geeze. Hey, I'm sorry you look like a geek."

"Rick!" Paloma exclaimed.

"Sorry." Rick hid his smile as he lowered his head.

Gabby stuck her tongue out at Rick and pulled a face. "My friends think I look great."

"Compared to what?" Rick shot back, his expression saying he couldn't resist.

"Shutup," Gabby returned.

"I won't," Rick spat.

"You're just stupid. You don't know anything." Gabby squinted her eyes angrily and puckered her lips as she shook her head at him.

Rick shrugged. "Well, I know what looks good and you sure don't."

"Okay, that's enough. Both of you," Raul interjected when he felt the bickering had gone far enough.

Paloma tried not to laugh. After all, Gabby had stood up for herself. She hadn't caved in and run from the room. She'd stood up for what she believed, even if it was not conventional. "If Gabby likes her style, then we will respect that."

Rick threw a stunned look at Paloma and Raul, as if he couldn't believe his ears. "What would you do if I came to breakfast dressed like that?" he asked Raul.

"We're not talking about you, young man. We're talking about Gabby."

Gabby stuck her tongue out again.

"You'd better keep that in your mouth unless you want to lose it."

"Rick," Raul warned.

"Sorry."

Paloma began to clear the table and rinse the dishes for the dishwasher. "Want to help me?" she asked Gabby.

"Sure."

"Stack the plates and scrape them into the garbage disposal. Then put them in the dishwasher."

The dishes in the washer and the kitchen cleaned from breakfast, Paloma and Gabby set off for the construction site at the Timberland.

"You really a plumber?"

"Sure am. Licensed by the State of Michigan."

"Hmm."

"My grandfather was a plumber. He started the business right after he and my grandmother got married. He was a migrant worker and saved money for years to own his own business. He also sent money to Mexico to his family. He had ten brothers and sisters and he was the oldest. He tells stories of standing in line every Saturday at the post office, waiting to buy a money order."

"Does he still have family in Mexico?"

"He does. We go visit at least once a year. He tried to get his mother to move up here after his father died, but she wouldn't hear of it. She lived there until her death. But he still has several brothers and sisters there."

"I'd like to see Mexico. My family is from Mexico too."

"Really?" Paloma studied her.

"My mother told me before she died that my real mother insisted that the family that adopted me be Spanish and Catholic. So I figure I must have Spanish relatives somewhere."

Paloma was at a loss. This child wanted to know about her real family. If only she could tell her the truth.

❦

"What's this going to be?" Gabby leaned out the window as they drove past the vast construction of the rustic log lodge.

"It's going to be a resort with a golf course, a main lodge made of hand-hewn logs and several small log cottages that people will rent."

"And you're going to plumb it all?"

"My crew will." She pulled the truck into the lot beside Raul's. "I have a ten man crew. I mainly oversee the work and draw up the prints, do the ordering and things like that."

Gabby nodded. "You're the boss?"

Paloma laughed. "I guess you could say that."

"Hey, Gabby. Wanna come ride the crane?" Rick rushed in. "Bill says he'll give us a ride before he begins lifting the logs."

"Sure. Can I?" Gabby asked Paloma in a surprisingly polite manner that showed her adoptive mother had instilled some manners.

"Sure. But be careful."

The two ran off toward the large piece of machinery, trying to outrun each other.

"It don't look too bad, does it?" Raul strolled beside her.

Paloma watched her daughter laugh and apparently enjoy herself as the crane driver demonstrated his job. "I don't think she's as bad as her adoptive father led us to believe. She just needs a little love and understanding, that's all."

"I made coffee in the office. Care for some?" Raul offered.

Paloma followed him into the little trailer. "I ordered the furnaces today. They should be here sometime the first of the week." She pulled the door closed behind her. "Carl went downstate for a few days, I'm told."

"Yeah, I heard that too. I don't think he'll be too happy when he finds out you married me."

"No, I don't suppose he will be. But it was over before it began. We had nothing in common but work."

Raul poured a steaming cup of coffee and handed it to her. "I hope we have more in common than that." A grin turned the corners of his mouth.

"Oh, I don't know..." she teased in return.

Raul turned serious. "She's going to be all right, don't you think?"

Paloma sipped the coffee. "I think so. She just needs to fit in somewhere, to belong. We'll help her. And Rick? Have you ever seen the like? He can say what he thinks and she takes it?"

Raul laughed. I know. I could have throttled him when he said what he said at breakfast, but she took it like you said. I think Rick will be good for her."

Paloma nodded. "I think so too."

The phone rang, interrupting their discussion. Paloma settled back in the chair as Raul answered the call.

"The project is moving along faster than I expected. We'll be outta here before Thanksgiving." He winked at Paloma. "Yes, sir. Things are going along better than I planned. If there are any changes, I'll let you know, otherwise, I'll see you in a couple of weeks." He hung up the receiver.

"That was the owner."

"I suspected as much. He's coming here?"

"In a few weeks to inspect the place. I think he'll be very pleased at the progress."

"I can say for sure the plumbing and heating are well ahead of schedule. If things keep going..."

Raul took the coffee cup from her hand. "Paloma..."

She looked deeply into his eyes and felt herself drowning. "Raul..." She could hear the wild pounding of her heart.

He reached out and gently took her face between his hands, bent his head and swept her away with his kiss.

Shivers of passion ignited and flowed through her like molten lava. Her senses were reeling. "We shouldn't be doing this."

He lifted her from the chair and gently laid her on the carpeting. "And why not? You're my wife."

"Someone might walk in."

He reached to his right and flipped the door lock. "There…no one can come in now." His lips claimed hers again. The kiss deepened, sweeping her away to a world so old and primitive, a world where lovers have gone since the beginning of time.

He lifted his head and stared at her. "Do you know what you do to me? Fireworks and the Fourth of July wouldn't do justice to how I feel about you." His voice was thick with passion. Ignoring any of the sounds of construction outside, they rode the wind tides with the eagles. They were in a world of their own, a world where only they existed.

Some time later Paloma sat on the rug, buttoning her shirt. "I must look a mess."

Raul kissed her nose. "A prettier mess, I've never seen." He laughed.

She rose to her feet. "I have to get back to work. It's going to be a long day."

Raul stood beside her. "I know. But it could be as long a night."

Paloma grew serious. "I know. Gabby and I have to start packing when we get back home."

"Rick and I will be there to move the heavy things."

"I know. It's going to take longer than one night. We'll just get my personal things tonight and we can gradually get the rest later."

He bent and kissed her softly on the mouth. "You better get back to work before I forget myself again." He patted her on the backside as she unlatched the door, took her hard hat and left.

That night they started moving Paloma's things into Raul's house. Gabby and Rick did their part in helping. Each day, Gabby went to work with Paloma and in the afternoon packed and moved more things. Little by little she toned down her shocking dress. First the ring in her eyebrow disappeared, and then the nose ring. Next the black leather attire was replaced with jeans, a tee shirt and a pair of sneakers. And lastly, her pretty face was scrubbed clean of all the punk makeup.

"Kids!" Paloma called from the deck of her new home as the steaks sizzled on the grill.

"Coming," they cried in unison, running at breakneck speed, each trying to beat the other to the deck.

"Careful," Paloma cautioned. "We don't want any accidents."

"Is dinner ready?" Rick asked, totally out of breath.

"Not quite. Raul and I have something to discuss with you."

"What?"

"We were thinking since the project is coming along so well, we'd like to take a long weekend and go up to the cabin for a while. What do you say?"

"Radical," Gabby answered in her childish voice, using a word left over from her rebellious period.

"When we goin'?" Rick asked.

Raul sauntered out from the kitchen with a bowl of salad in his hands. "How about next weekend?"

So soon, Paloma thought. She had to prepare her grandparents for their great-grandchild. However was she going to do that? No matter how many times she had rehearsed what to say, it sounded stupid each time. What could she say? "Gram, Pop, I'd like you to meet the child I gave up eleven years ago. The child I conceived out of wedlock and never told you about."

"You look sad. Is anything wrong?" Raul leaned toward her as if he felt her distress.

Paloma shook her head. "No, I was just thinking."

He squeezed her arm reassuringly and winked. "I know. But it's going to be okay."

"Hey, the steaks are burning!" Rick yelled as he lifted the lid of the gas grill.

Gabby followed his gaze. "They are not. But they are done," she warned.

"Who'd like to go shopping tomorrow?" Paloma asked as they were cleaning up from dinner.

"What for?" Rick dumped his paper plate and cup into the plastic bag.

"If we're going on a little trip, we need a few new things... you know, clothes, things we might need for the great northern wilderness."

"Naw." Rick shook his head. "Not unless you get me a new fishing pole and some grubs, but I don't think you know much about that."

Oh, really, Paloma thought. Little do you know, son. Keeping a straight face, she said, "Well, then perhaps Gabby and I'll go and you guys can fend for yourselves. She threw a wink in Raul's direction."

❦

"How do you like this?" Paloma held up a brown top that matched a pair of geometrical designed shorts.

"It's all right," Gabby said but her face brightened when she saw something else. "But I really like these." She held up a pair of black shorts and top.

"If you really like them, I'll get them for you."

"Really?"

Paloma nodded. "I said so and I always keep my word." Oh, Lord, she was testing again. Would it ever stop?

Gabby carried the two-piece garment around and then put it back. "How about these?" She held up a pair of denim cutoffs and a white, short-sleeved shirt with tiny blue flowers around the collar.

"I like it." Paloma worked at keeping acceptance from her tone. She was going to let Gabby make certain decisions on her own and if they were wrong, then so be it.

Gabby nodded. "I like them." She placed them in the basket Paloma was carrying.

They went through the store buying bathing suits and casual summerwear for both of them, as well as beach towels, thongs, sun blocker and several other things.

"How about this for Raul?" Paloma held up an olive green shirt that said, I can talk the talk because I can walk the walk.

"That's crazy." Gabby turned up her nose at the shirt with white lettering.

But Paloma put the shirt in her cart, knowing Raul would know what the saying meant even if it had gone over Gabby's head. She found a Detroit Tigers baseball shirt and hat she felt Rick would like. Then decided on a couple of No Fear shirts as well.

Since Paloma had a mountain bike, she got both Gabby and Rick a bike. If Rick didn't like his, he could exchange it. What about Raul? She didn't know if he had one or not, but she'd find out.

To top the afternoon off, she bought Rick a fishing rod, reel, a box of hooks and a tin of grubs. There, that ought to show him, she thought, satisfied with her purchases. She helped Gabby pick out her own pole and tackle box.

"What did you girls do today?" Raul came in looking exhausted.

"You look tired. Hard day?" Paloma met him and kissed him gently.

Raul slumped on the sofa. "It couldn't be worse. The crane broke down and we had to get a mechanic. That put us a little behind, but not bad."

"We went shopping." Gabby shyly spoke from her television watching position on the floor.

"What'd you get?" Raul asked.

"Everything is out on the table. Go look." Gabby pointed to the dining room.

"Get that special bag." Paloma gave Gabby a secretive smile.

"Hey." Rick raced into the room. "You guys went shopping." He looked at the purchases laid out on the table.

"I asked you to go, remember?" Paloma reminded him.

"Yeah, I remember."

"Here, how do you like this?" She handed him the bags and boxes she got for him.

"Gee whiz." He fell to the floor, his arms loaded with the packages. He held up the baseball shirt and hat. "Wow! How'd you know?" He tore into the other packages and exclaimed over each shirt.

"Here." Paloma handed him the long package wrapped in brown paper and string. "This is from the girl who doesn't know much about fishing."

"Oh my gosh!" He pulled the paper from the Shakespeare rod. "And a Chimino reel. I've always wanted a reel like this. How'd you know?"

"There's more." She handed him the smaller packages.

He glanced up from the tin of grubs, a sheepish grin pasted to his face. "I'm sorry. You know a lot about fishing." He ran his hand over the thin rod and put the reel back in its box.

"And there's a surprise waiting for you in the garage. Gabby will show you."

"What about me?" Raul leaned against the archway. "Didn't I get anything?"

Paloma picked up the green plastic bag and tossed it at him. He narrowed his eyes and peeked cautiously into the bag. His laugh was rich as pulled the shirt from the bag. "Is this what you think of me?"

"Oh, I don't know. I just thought it was you. She picked up the wrappings that lay on the floor and twisted them into one neat bundle. "There's another one in there too. I couldn't resist."

He pulled out the black shirt that read, No conceit in my family, I've got it all.

He chuckled and said, "Wait until I go shopping for you."

"Hey, Dad. You oughta see the bike Paloma got me."

"You sure shot your wad today, didn't you?" Raul teased.

Paloma shrugged. "We're going on vacation, after all. We needed things."

"Like this shirt?"

"Like that shirt."

"Are we going to stay at your grandfather's cabin?" Rick interrupted their gentle bantering.

"Actually, there's two cabins there. One my grandfather stays in because it's the one he feels more comfortable in, and a more modern one with three bedrooms and a loft." We'll stay there."

"I thought we might go camping," Rick lamented.

"I have an idea." Paloma knelt between Gabby and Rick. "There are a lot of camping things at my grandfather's house. Why don't you kids go through the stuff and see what you can come up with to take with us." She handed them her set of keys. "You both have a set of wheels. But be careful. Watch for cars," she called out.

The two scurried off through the kitchen. The back door closed with a resounding bang.

Paloma plopped down on the sofa beside Raul. "This is a lot of work."

"Handling kids always is."

"Mmm." She closed her eyes, exhaustion washing over her.

"What's for dinner?" he asked.

Paloma shot up. "Good Lord, I was so busy shopping I forgot all about dinner."

Raul pulled her back against him, his arm around her. "Never mind. I'm taking you and the kids out for dinner. You've had a very big day."

"Where we going?"

"Where do you want to go?"

She yawned. "I don't know." She yawned again. "Ask the kids when they get back."

Gently, he slid his arm from around her, put the pillow under her head and covered her with the afghan from the back of the sofa. She looked almost like a child with her hair falling over one shoulder and wispy tendrils framing her face. Long curving lashes lay against the creamy skin above her cheek bones. Was that the beginning of a smile on her slightly parted lips? What was she dreaming? Was it about him?

He couldn't resist. He reached out and without thinking caressed the hair away from her face.

She sighed a throaty moan, almost the purr of a kitten.

He stepped away. He didn't want to wake her. But she was so beautiful, he just wanted to take her in his arms and hold her forever. Instead of waking as he feared, she snuggled under the afghan and sighed deeply in sleep.

❦

The next thing Paloma heard was the clinking of plates and silverware. She sat up and removed the afghan. Where was she? What time was it? She glanced at her watch. Seven. She had to get the cobwebs out of her brain.

Seven! Dinner! She jumped to her feet.

"Hey, you're finally awake." Rick peeked at her from the dining room. "We thought you'd sleep forever."

"Dinner's served," Raul called.

"What dinner?" She rose from the sofa and yawned.

"Raul got Chinese," Gabby answered.

"Chinese. Mmm, smells good." Paloma made her way to the kitchen. "Let me wash my hands and I'll join you." She stopped. "Did you kids wash your hands?"

"Do you think Dad would let us help without washing our hands?" Rick held out clean hands toward her.

"Sorry."

"What did you get?" She peeked into the boxes.

Raul held her chair and seated himself across from her. "Pepper steak, garlic chicken, almond chicken, plain ol' chop suey with fried rice, and crab rangoons, because I know how much you like them."

"No egg rolls?"

Raul smiled and pointed at the oblong box.

"Not that I need them. I'm sure they're full of fat." Paloma could almost taste the delicious smelling food.

"Can Gabby and I eat in the living room and watch cable?"

Paloma pulled a frown. "I don't think its a good thing to eat in the living room, but if you're really careful, I'll let you just this once."

"Great," they cried in unison. They took their plates and disappeared through the archway.

"Looks like we're alone."

"Not often enough." Raul poured her a cup of tea.

"Shh." She glanced toward the living room, but there was no way the kids could hear him. The television was blaring loud action music. "The kids might hear you."

Raul laughed. "I don't think they can hear anything with that music blaring." He rose from his chair, came around to her side of the table and pulled her into his arms and backed them both into the shadowy kitchen.

"Dinner..." she murmured.

"You're dinner enough for me." His mouth found hers hungrily.

"Raul, the kids."

His mouth lightly pressed against hers. "They're busy with the television. Do you think they'll miss us?" His mouth trailed down her throat to the swell above the vee in her blouse. "You're my wife, Paloma, I can't forget that. Can you?"

"No..." she whispered, her head spinning as the blood raced through her body. He wanted her as much as she wanted to give herself to him.

They moved up the back stairway to their bedroom. She surrendered because she loved him. Needed him as much as he needed her. Again, as it always was with them, the world disappeared.

Chapter Ten

The day for the trip finally arrived. The double-cab truck was packed to the limit with suitcases and camping gear. Four bikes were affixed to the back. They left at six in the morning and were crossing the Big Mac bridge that spanned the upper and lower peninsulas of Michigan at seven. Gabby and Rick leaned forward to watch the glowing sun spreading its spell over the waters of the Straits of Mackinac.

"There's Mackinac Island over there." Paloma pointed to the right.

"Do people live there?" Gabby wanted to know.

Paloma nodded. "A lot of people live there, but they can't have any cars."

"Why not?"

"Because the island has always been a tourist hideaway. They've had a no-car rule for years and years. There are only horse and carriages or bicycles used for transportation."

"She's kidding, right?" Rick punched Raul in the right shoulder.

Raul shook his head. "Nope. Afraid she's right this time."

"Can we go there some time?" Gabby asked. "It sounds romantic."

"Yeah, right. As if you need any romance," Rick teased.

"Shut up!"

"Will not."

Paloma listened in satisfaction to the way Gabby was beginning to open up to everyone. Thank goodness those grunge clothes were a thing of the past, at least it seemed so.

"See that long white building over to the left? That's the Grand Hotel." Paloma reflected on her dreams of a long leisurely honeymoon, candlelit dinners, long walks along the shore and nights filled with unending passion.

Crossing the bridge from the Lower Peninsula to the Upper Peninsula was like entering another state. Large rock walls greeted them on the other side of the bridge just as they turned West on Highway 2.

The ribbon of asphalt wound along the shore of Lake Michigan, where white caps licked at the pebbled and sand beach. Opposite the lake were dense thickets of tangled trees and shrubs where one could only imagine the abundant variety of wildlife hidden from view.

The further they drove, the denser the woodland became. They were surrounded by tall evergreens that rose majestically on either side. Adding to the north's beauty were the clumps of birches that flashed white along the winding road, in stark contrast to the dark, almost black evergreens. Then they would come to the shore again with only one side of the road lined with ancient timberland.

Paloma glanced in the backseat and poked Raul in the ribs, motioning toward the kids. He glanced in the mirror and smiled. The gentle sparing had stopped. Gabby and Rick were curled around their pillows fast asleep. Somewhere between the bridge and the wilderness, they had fallen asleep.

"So much for staying awake to see every inch of the Upper Peninsula."

"They'll see it on the way back. If they stay awake." Raul threw her a smile.

"You know," Paloma reflected, "Finnish people settled here a hundred years or more. They came here from the old country to work the timber and the copper mines."

"Land of the lumberjacks and miners?"

"Timber played a very important part of life in northern Michigan for years. Of course, there are the copper mines up near Kewanaw and that little ghost town of Fayette that used to be a bustling pig iron company town on the Garden Peninsula."

Raul cracked his window to let in a little air. "I wish we had time to go to the Kewanaw Peninsula. I hear there are some great lighthouses along the Lake Superior shore.

"Maybe after the project is finished we could go for a while. Perhaps spend a week following the Superior shore and coming back along Lake Michigan, stopping to visit all the historical attractions."

"The kids would love that."

Paloma looked straight ahead when she said, "Maybe the kids won't be with us."

Raul threw a questioning glance in her direction. "You mean there is a chance in this lifetime when I just might have you all to myself?"

A mischievous frown flitted across her features. "You sound selfish, Mr. Fernandez."

"No, just impatient for a honeymoon that seems long overdue, Mrs. Fernandez."

Paloma glanced down at the shiny wedding ring on her finger. It was strange, she didn't really feel married. Of course she was married, she knew that. It was just that there had been no romance and excitement in it.

Oh, there had been the times they could steal away and have a few stolen moments together. But it was just like this trip. The kids were always there and it had to be that way, she knew. But that didn't stop her from longing for time alone with Raul.

"How far is your place from the bridge?"

"About an hour and a half, I'd say. It's about ten miles north of Indian Lake."

Raul rolled his window down a little more. "Do you realize that just a few weeks ago it was spitting snow and now it really looks and feels like spring?"

"It happens that way up here."

"Do you know what my dream is?" Raul asked.

Paloma shook her head.

"I would love to have a place up here for six months and another place in the south to spend the winter. Maybe Florida. My family came from Little Havana, you know."

Paloma laughed. "Or maybe Mexico. It's very inexpensive to live there. And it's so beautiful and warm in the winter."

"Maybe. Who knows." He shot her a questioning glance. "Perhaps we will spend a little time in both places. Visit my family and then visit yours."

"I'd like a place of our own," she said thoughtfully.

"That too." He nodded. "We can have two places, can't we?"

"If you say so." She smiled. "Do you think we'd miss all the snow and winter festivities? I'm sure the kids would."

"We could fly back for a ski weekend. When we've had enough, back we'd go. What do you think of that?"

Paloma glanced at him from under her long lashes. "You have things all figured out, it seems."

"Only if it's all right with you. But I do hate the winters, at least being here all winter long."

Paloma squeezed his arm. "I know. I was just teasing you. I've never loved the long winters myself. My heart is in the South, warm sunshine and palm trees." She gazed out the window.

"There's a pasty place. Let's stop at the next one and take some pasties to the cabin for dinner. There's nothing like Upper Peninsula pasties." Paloma pointed to the quaint yellow building that boasted the best homemade pasties in the North. "The recipe is supposed to have come from the Finnish who made these little meat pies to take to work."

Raul turned the car around in the middle of the empty road. "Why not stop right now and get what you want. We might miss the next one."

Rick roused just enough to see where they were and went back to sleep. Gabby never moved.

Paloma got her pasties and a container of both beef and chicken gravy. "I hope the kids like them. I used to look forward to coming up and having these when I was a kid."

"We've got some hot dogs in the cooler if they don't," Raul said.

"Gram makes a great pasty from a recipe that she got from an elderly neighbor who claims it came from some ancestor who used to live in the Upper. Anyway, no matter how she tries, and they are delicious mind you, they just aren't the same as what you get up here."

"Maybe it's the novelty of coming to the great outdoors and getting them where they originated."

He was probably right. She remembered the good times when she was a kid without a care in the world, remembered how excited she was to be going to their north woods cabin. "That's it exactly. I remember how I felt whenever we came north."

Raul left Highway 2 at Manistique. The sun was shining brightly and a gentle breeze played through the tops of the tall trees lining both sides of the road. There was still a nip in the air for the first of May, but this was northern Michigan.

"Are we there yet?" Gabby woke rubbing her eyes.

"Just a few more miles," Paloma answered.

Raul turned the truck onto a dirt road, one so rutted and full of holes he was careful to drive slow. Tall, commanding evergreens lined both sides of the long drive. Heavy cedar boughs brushed the sides of the car as they drove past.

"You'd think your grandfather would have this road widened."

"Not on your life." Paloma laughed. "This is his private little paradise."

"Are we lost?" Gabby glanced out at the dense forest on both sides of them.

Paloma shook her head. "No. This is just part of being in the great north woods."

"I don't know if I like it or not."

"Oh, stop being a scaredy-cat," Rick chided her.

"I'm not scared. I just don't like spooky, dark woods."

Before the kids could argue any more, they rounded a sharp curve and came through a small clearing. Straight ahead was a small lake and nestled to the left under several, sheltering northern white pines, was a rustic cabin with a screened-in front porch.

"Just behind that cabin is the new one." Paloma pointed. "Just keep driving and you'll pull right in front of it."

The drive was carpeted with pine needles, making their approach almost soundless except for the gentle hum of the motor. It was exactly as she'd remembered it from the last time. The new cabin was more modern. Really, it was a house.

"Now this is an unexpected turn of events." Raul maneuvered the Bronco up to the house through a tight stand of birch trees. "I didn't expect this."

"Why? I told you how modern it was."

He thrust his hands through his hair. "I know you did. But I thought you were seeing this whole place through the eyes of a child."

"Thanks a lot."

Amusement danced in his eyes. "No, no. I meant you'd always loved this place, so I thought you naturally blew it up better than it was." He unfolded himself from the vehicle and stretched.

"Can we go to the lake?" Rick scrambled from the backseat, followed by Gabby.

"Yes, but be careful. And don't fall in, the water's still very cold," she called after them.

"Raul...?"

"You want to speak to your grandparents alone. I'll keep the kids busy and unpack."

"Thanks." She leaned forward and kissed him on the cheek. But he didn't release her. His mouth crushed hers with heated promises for later.

"I'll remember that." She touched her finger to his lips and disappeared through the thick growth that separated the two cabins. Glancing back, she saw he was still standing there watching her.

Paloma quietly stepped into the kitchen of the cabin through the back door and was instantly greeted by the delicious smell of her grandmother's cooking.

"Gram," she whispered. "Where's Pop?"

"Oh, *nina.* I've missed you." Her grandmother hugged her. "He's on the porch."

"Inez..." Pop's voice echoed from the front porch. "There're a couple of kids playing on our beach. Find out who they are and tell them this is private property."

"I'll see to Pop." She kissed her grandmother on the cheek. "I have to talk to him...I have to tell you both something."

Inez smiled and inclined her head. "I know that look. It means you're troubled."

"It's not as bad as you think. I just want to tell you both about something that happened a long time ago. I hope you can understand and forgive me."

"Forgive you? There's nothing in this world I could not forgive you. Now come along before your grandfather has a fit."

"Inez!" His voice bellowed from the porch. "Who are those kids?"

"They're with me." Paloma moved slowly onto the porch, her grandmother close behind.

"Paloma, *nina*. What are you doing here?" Mex swiveled his wheelchair around, surprise in his face.

"I came to see you and Gram, why else?"

He turned and glanced at the shore. "Who are those kids?"

She took a deep, nervous breath. She pulled one of the natural tone wicker chairs close to his. "I've got something to talk to you about and...you too, Gram. Come sit down." She motioned to the other chair.

He reached out his hand. "What is it? Has something gone sour on the job...a problem you can't handle?"

Paloma shook her head. "No, nothing like that. In fact, the job is ahead of schedule."

He still held her hands. He fingered her wedding ring and raised questioning eyes to hers. "Is Carl with you?"

She colored. "No. Not Carl." She pulled her hands away and nervously rose to her feet. She stood staring out at the kids racing up and down the sand.

"Paloma. You know you can tell me anything, tell us anything. You're upset. Now tell us what's wrong."

"Pop, this story started a long, long time ago, when I was in college."

"College? So long ago and whatever it is still upsets you?"

"It upsets me that I have to tell you something I did and I don't want you to be ashamed of me. I did what I did because I never wanted to bring shame to our family. I need you to understand." Her voice broke.

"We'd never be ashamed of you. Now come sit down and tell us everything." His voice was warm, inviting and coaxing. Her grandmother sat quietly in the chair, her hands folded tightly in her lap.

"Well, when I was a freshman in college I met someone and fell deeply in love."

"In love? You never told your grandmother or me." He glanced at his wife then at Paloma.

Her brows drew together in an agonized expression. "I was going to. We planned a trip north and then I got a visit from his ex-girlfriend who told me she was pregnant and they were getting back together."

"And you found each other again, is that it?"

"Well, sort of."

"Bring the young man in. I'd like to meet the man who won my *nina's* heart."

"There's more to it than that and this is the hard part. I need both of you to understand." She wiped the threatening tears from her eyes. "I got pregnant."

"Pregnant?" he exclaimed. "When? How? We never knew."

Paloma shook her head. "I made sure you never knew. Remember when I had extra classes that summer and I couldn't come home? I stayed behind to have the baby."

"Paloma. Why didn't you tell us?" Disillusioned hurt edged each word.

"I knew how you and Gram felt about that sort of thing. I didn't want to bring disgrace on the family. And the father, he didn't know either. I never told him."

"So? What did you do with the baby?" her grandmother barely got the question out.

She hiccuped a sob. "I gave it up for adoption."

Her grandfather lowered his head in his hands. "Oh, Paloma, Paloma, what did we do to you?" He raised pained eyes to her. "We instilled strict morals in you, yes. But we never intended for you to go through something like this and never let us know. We should have been there for you. You needed us. Inez?"

Tears streamed down her grandmother's face. "You should have come to us. We would have helped." She rose and moved to the windows to watch the children.

"I know. I was so young, so afraid. I couldn't tell. So I did the next best thing...or so I thought. I insisted the baby be placed with a Spanish and Catholic family. I knew you would approve of that much at least."

"So, why tell us all this now?" her grandfather asked.

She paced the floor, biting her lower lip. This was the most difficult thing she had ever done in her life. Her nerves screamed from the tension.

"I've lived with this secret for twelve years. You don't know how many times I've wanted to tell you, but I couldn't. After I met the father again, I had to find the baby."

She turned to her grandfather. "Not to try to gain custody or anything like that, but to know she was all right. I had to know she had a good home, but I found out different."

"What happened?"

"Her adoptive mother died last year and her adoptive father didn't want her, had never wanted her."

He leaned back in his chair and sat quietly as she told them the trouble Gabby had gotten into and how she had gotten custody of the girl only by marrying the biological father.

"And who is this elusive father?"

"Raul Fernandez."

"Fernandez!" he exclaimed. "That explains your dislike of him at first. Now you're married to him. And those children?"

"The girl is Gabby, our daughter, and the boy is Rick, Raul's son from his first marriage."

He sat and nodded. "Do you think it will work out? Will you be happy, really happy with this arrangement?"

She knelt in front of his chair. "I'm happy right now, Pop. Raul loves me, really loves me. And he wants to make us a family, a real family. I know there's a lot of work to be done with Gabby to get her head on straight, but it'll all work out in time."

"That's it then. There's nothing more to be said."

"What?" Paloma stared at him in disbelief. "What do you mean?"

He reached out and ran her thick braid through his fingers. "You're happy. That's all I ever wanted for you. If you're happy, I'm happy. Nothing else matters."

She threw herself into his arms and kissed him on the cheek. "Oh, thank you, Pop. Thanks for everything."

"*Sí*." her grandmother said quietly. "You must be happy." Her faded eyes turned to her. "You married in the church?"

"No."

Her grandmother crossed herself and closed her eyes. "That is the first thing you must do. You must be married in the church. Your marriage must be blessed by a priest." She gasped. "This man of yours. He is Catholic, isn't he?"

"I think so."

"You think so? Don't you know?"

"We've not discussed it."

Again her grandmother crossed herself. "I must light another candle and pray." She left the porch.

Paloma made to follow but her grandfather stayed her. "No. Let her go. Give her time to think all this over. This has been a shock to her."

"I know. I'm sorry."

"When do I get to meet these kids of yours?"

"As soon as I can run them down. But remember, Gabby doesn't know I'm her mother."

He shook his head. "Don't worry. I won't tell her a thing."

"Mind if I intrude?" Raul sauntered onto the porch from the cabin.

"Raul." Mex held out his hand. "Welcome to the family."

Raul took his hand. "I assume Paloma has filled you and Mrs. Espinoza in on everything."

"She has."

"I hope you understand."

Mex looked at them both. "She says you love her? Do you?"

Raul reached out and pulled Paloma close to him. "More than anything in the world."

Mex nodded. "That's all that counts. But I expect you to take good care of her for the rest of her life."

"I will, sir. I promise."

"That's one promise I expect you to keep."

"Pop..." Paloma threw him a pleading look.

Raul glanced down at her. "It's all right. He loves you as much as I do. It's natural he wants to make sure you'll be happy. And sir, I give you that promise."

"I want to ask you something else too."

"What is that, sir."

"Are you Catholic?"

"Was baptized and raised Catholic, yes."

"Paloma tells us you were not married by a priest."

"There was no time. A judge married us."

"Then there must be another wedding, in the church and blessed by the priest."

Raul turned to Paloma. "Will you have me, again?"

"Well, now, I don't know," she teased.

"Paloma!" her grandfather sternly warned.

She held up her hands in a sign of peace. "Just kidding, just kidding."

"Good. Everything is settled."

"Paloma." Rick and Gabby called as they raced toward the house waving their arms excitedly.

"Kids, I'd like you to meet my grandfather. This is Gabby, and this is Rick." She placed a hand on the shoulder of each of the kids.

"Hi," both kids said in unison. "Paloma, there's an island in the middle of the lake. Can we go there sometime?"

Paloma laughed. "Yes, but someone will have to go with you."

The kids were jumping up and down, hardly able to stand still. "We gotta go. There's so much to explore."

"Be careful and don't go too far," Paloma called after them.

"They seem like nice kids," Mex observed.

"They are." Paloma gazed after them proudly. "It'll take time for Gabby to really adjust, especially after we tell her we're her parents, but I have a good feeling about everything."

Paloma and Raul took the loft bedroom. Gabby had a room of her own and so did Rick, both on the first floor with a bathroom between.

The day had been pleasant, and even though the evening turned cool, they left the door facing the lake open. A fire crackled pleasantly in the stone fireplace and snapped as the pine burned, sending red-gold sparks up the chimney. Her home in Petoskey was quiet compared to the city, but here in the far north, it was different. It was as if everything and everyone were at one with nature.

Outside a lonesome owl hooted into the darkening night, and the song of crickets and frogs promised the renewal of life's constant cycle.

Paloma sat on the oval braided rug in front of the fire, cradled in Raul's strong arms. Watching the hypnotic glow of yellow-orange flames she felt satisfied, pleasantly drowsy and complete. She was at peace for the first time in a very long time.

Raul leaned forward and found her lips. The night was magic, made for lovers.

"Do you know how long I've waited to do this?" His mouth took hers again in a deepening, passion-filled kiss.

She returned his passion, wrapping her arms around his neck. Locked in each other's arms, his tongue parted her lips, his hand found the buttons of her shirt and began unbuttoning them, to explore the soft mounds beneath.

"Hey, you guys. Look what I found." Rick bounded down the stairs holding a guitar in his hands.

Raul and Paloma rolled apart as if ice water had been dumped on them. Paloma hastily fastened her buttons and Raul leaned against the sofa, muttering, "Damn it anyway," under his breath.

"That used to be mine." Paloma fought for composure. "I played it once, a long time ago." She smiled, remembering the days she dreamed of having her own group and singing for the world. She kept her eyes averted from Raul. What timing! Why hadn't they used their heads? The kids were in the house. And the inevitable had happened.

"Can you play it?" Rick sat on the rug beside them, obviously unaware he had interrupted anything personal.

Paloma took the guitar and ran her fingers over the string. It needed tuning, but within seconds she had it sounding right.

"What's going on?" Gabby came down the steps in her bare feet and pajamas.

"Paloma's gonna play the guitar for us." Rick stretched on his stomach, his chin resting in his hands as he watched her fingers move over the strings.

Paloma played a few cords.

"Hey, you're good," Rick praised.

"I remember how well you used to sing. Sing for us," Raul asked, leaning back against the front of the sofa, his long legs stretched out before him, his hands folded behind his head, and resigned to playing the patient lover.

Paloma sang her favorite Leann Rimes song, "Blue," filling the room with warm music. Her sweet voice rose and fell. Moving smoothly from one song to another, she held everyone captive.

"Don't stop," Gabby begged, "you have a beautiful voice."

"Thank you," Paloma said, pleased that she'd found another thing on which to build a common bond with her daughter. "Sing along with me?" she invited.

Gabby shook her head, a tinge of color seeping into her cheeks. "I can't sing. My dad always said I sounded like a caterwauling cat."

Damn the man. Paloma fought not to show her hatred of the man who had demeaned her daughter. How could he have been so callous to the child he reared. "Oh, come on. I bet you can." Paloma plucked the guitar strings. "Listen to the music, then the words. I'll play and sing them again and you join me." She strummed a romantic, country song.

Paloma's clear voice once again rode on waves of silken enchantment. "Okay. Now, you sing with me." As she began singing, Gabby joined in, though in a timid voice barely audible.

"You have a very nice voice," Paloma encouraged. "Let's try it again, only louder this time."

Again they filled the room with song, Gabby singing a little louder, in a sweet young voice which complemented her mother's more mature, practiced one. Before long, she was singing with a zest to equal Paloma's, her shyness fading.

"Go, girl!" Rick encouraged, clapping his hands to the beat of the music.

"Gabby, you have a very lovely voice," Paloma said, meaning every word of the praise.

"Can we sing one of Selena's songs we saw on video?" Gabby asked.

Paloma strummed. "I don't know if I can do Selena. She is more pop. I think I'd have to practice her music. But don't worry, I'll teach you the words to the songs I know. Listen to the music first, then I'll sing the words."

On the second time through the song, Gabby followed along with Paloma. Closing her eyes, Gabby sang from her heart, obviously at one with the music. She's so much like I was at that age, Paloma thought.

When they finished, Gabby touched the guitar. "I wish I knew how to play."

"Want to learn?"

Gabby's eyes brightened, excitement dancing in her face. "You'd teach me?"

"Of course." Paloma handed her the instrument. "Put the strap over your shoulder and hold it like this." She leaned behind the girl, holding her fingers in place on the frets. "Now strum. Good. That was the A cord.

And this one," she placed Gabby's fingers on the strings in a different position, "is C."

"I think you're a natural for music, *nina*." Paloma leaned back and watched her daughter flawlessly repeat what she'd learned in the matter of minutes.

"Where did you learn to play?" Raul asked.

"Pop taught me. He used to sing and play when I was a kid. Then I decided I wanted to learn and Pop got me a guitar for my birthday one year."

"I wish I could play like you." Gabby gently stroked the strings, practicing the cords.

Paloma nodded. "Pop got me books for a beginner and I practiced and practiced until I could play almost as well as he could. I've always loved music."

"Me too." Gabby softly played, humming to the cords.

"I don't think the books are here, but I'll look. If they're not, I'll find them when we get home. You can have them and the guitar."

"Really? You'd give this to me?" She ran her hand lovingly over the polished wood of the instrument.

"Of course. I can always use yours when I get an itch to play. And if we want to play together, I can always buy another."

"Bitchin'!" Gabby exclaimed, reverting to her punk vocabulary.

Chapter Eleven

To the soft, soothing orchestra of northern woodland activity, Paloma and Raul lay curled in each other's arms, spent and satisfied. She listened to Raul's deep, even breathing. He was asleep. But she couldn't sleep. She was too filled with wonderment and satisfaction from their lovemaking.

Somewhere out in that dense, mysterious forest, a lone whippoorwill gave his lonely, haunting cry. She listened to the gentle lapping of the lake's water and stared at the silver rays of the moon filtering into the room. Her eyes grew heavier and heavier until they fluttered shut and she fell into a peaceful, exhausted sleep.

Childish laughter rode the early morning breeze, waking her. She yawned, stretched and felt emptiness beside her. Turning her head, she was disappointed to find Raul gone. Only the indentation on his pillow gave evidence he had been there.

She rose and stepped to the French doors, pulling curtains aside. On the dock that jetted out into the dark waters of the small lake stood Raul, helping Gabby with a fishing rod. Rick was reeling his in, yelling excitedly about having caught a big one.

"Darn," he exclaimed as the fish wiggled itself off his hook. "And it was a big one, too."

Raul laughed. "It's always the big ones that get away, son."

Paloma smiled, letting the curtains fall back into place. Everything was working out right. She and Raul were married. Gabby was coming around, and her grandparents had taken everything in stride. Of course her grandmother still was upset about her not being married in the church, but they would remedy that as soon as they returned home.

After a shower she slipped into a clean pair of jeans and a peach colored sweat shirt. Pulling her hair back, she clasped it at the nape of her neck and smiled into the full length mirror at her country girl reflection.

The smell of coffee wafted up to greet her as she moved down the steps, though there was no sign of breakfast. She stepped out onto the deck.

"Hey. How about a little breakfast?" she called.

"We're trying to catch some," Rick called back, waving.

"Right." She waved back. "If we wait for you guys, we'll starve. I'll start the bacon."

Soon the kitchen was filled with the warm smells of breakfast and the soft clatter of dishes as she finished setting the table.

"Come on. You can fish after breakfast," she called from the deck. "You don't want a cold meal, and I only cook once," she warned.

"Hey, fishing is bitchin'!" Gabby placed her rod outside on the deck and went to the kitchen sink to wash her hands.

Paloma closed her eyes, no longer able to hold her tongue. "Gabby." She pulled the girl to one side so no one would hear her. "I really don't like that word. Do you think you could find another to use in its place?"

Gabby lowered her head, color seeping into her face. "I'll try, I promise."

Paloma put her arms around her. "I'd appreciate it. It's not a very nice word and you're much too intelligent to use language like that."

"Smells great." Raul and Rick sauntered in looking every bit the fishermen, with their vests decorated with hooks and small lures.

"It's ready." Paloma placed the hot syrup on the table and sat down with her family.

"I called the construction site on my cell phone and everything is going good." Raul took pancakes and bacon as Paloma poured him a cup of coffee.

"And the mechanics? Did you ask how my crew is coming along?"

Raul nodded. "Carl isn't back yet, but my man said they are ahead of schedule and everything looks good."

Paloma was relieved. Her family came first but that didn't stop her from worrying about the job. This bit of news gave her time to enjoy her little vacation and build a family bond.

"So, I was thinking." Raul glanced at everyone. "How'd you like to go to Fayette tomorrow?'

"What's Fayette?" Gabby asked.

"Well, you're in for a treat." Raul leaned toward her with his fork in his hand. "Fayette is a ghost town left over from the days when pig iron was big business. The State of Michigan is working to bring it back like it was when it was a bustling company town."

"What's there?" Rick piped up.

"The old three-story hotel, the doctor's office, several buildings that used to be the company offices, the opera house and several restored homes with period furniture. We can see how the people lived at that time."

"Sounds boring to me." Rick groaned.

"Aren't you interested in history?"

Rick's face reflected apathy. "I get enough of that in school."

Raul ignored his son and continued, "And I was thinking on our way home we might go to Mackinac Island and spend the night. How's that?"

"Now that sounds like fun. Can I ride a horse?"

"Me, too," chimed in Gabby. "I've never ridden a horse before."

"We'll all ride horses and bikes too, if you want."

"Can we go fishing again?" Rick finished his milk.

"Go ahead. But be careful not to fall in. The water's still cold," Paloma warned as the kids rushed out the sliding door.

Raul watched them race down the path to the dock. "They're great kids, aren't they?"

Paloma nodded. "And Rick is so good for Gabby. She's coming out of that self-imposed shell she protected herself with."

"I think she's going to be all right." Raul stared after her. "I just wish I had been able to watch her grow up."

"Me too."

"Oh, well. We have the rest of her life. But I worry about telling her about us," Raul murmured.

"We have to wait until we're very sure she's able to handle it." Paloma rose and linked her arm in his.

"That's the tricky part. How are we going to know?"

Paloma shrugged. "I guess we'll know when the time comes."

Raul helped her clear the table and scrape the food scraps into the garbage. "You know, I was thinking that if your grandfather will let me, I'll take the kids out in his boat fishing. Do you think he'd mind?"

Paloma shook her head. "Of course not. But you can go over and ask him while I finish cleaning the kitchen."

"Want to come with us?" He paused at the door.

"Not this time. You need time alone with the kids. I have a few things to do here and then I'll go visit Pop and Gram for a while. You go and have a good time."

Raul moved across the kitchen and pulled her into the warm circle of his arms. "You're a very special person."

His mouth teased hers and with a moan she open hers. Fire swept through her and her heart pounded wildly.

"Sweet, sweet Paloma, he whispered against her lips. "I can't seem to get enough of you."

Closing her eyes, she swayed with him, feeling all the glorious sensations of passion. His hand moved under her sweatshirt to her soft middrift causing her skin to tingle.

She gently pushed him away. "If you keep this up, there'll be no fishing this morning."

He kissed her again and reluctantly pulled away. "I know, but you feel so good."

"Later," she whispered. "Later."

"I'll consider that a promise I intend to hold you to." He winked and walked away.

She felt strangely empty, wanting more. Get hold of yourself, she chided herself. There's lots to do today to keep busy. Just remember tonight and all the nights in the future.

Paloma washed the dishes and put them away. She swept the decks and leaned on the railing watching the trio in the boat fishing out toward the island. Laughter filtered to shore along with the excited, muffled voices of Rick and Gabby as they both caught a fish.

"They sound like a happy lot." Inez pulled her sweater around her and joined Paloma on the deck.

Paloma turned to her grandmother. "What are you doing?"

"I decided to take a little walk, to think. Then I heard all the laughter and decided to give you a little visit."

Paloma put her arm around her grandmother and watched her family. "They do sound happy."

"I hope you, Raul and the children will come and have dinner with Pop and me tonight."

Paloma's face fell slightly. "I'd really like to, but the kids are expecting to eat any fish they might catch."

Inez nodded. "I know and I told Raul earlier I'd fix them and a little something else just in case."

They both laughed, knowing the fickleness of fishing.

"All right. It sounds wonderful, but you must let me help."

Inez glanced at the boat, then back to Paloma. "And what if they get a good catch?"

"Then, we eat what we've prepared tomorrow. Better safe than sorry." Paloma linked her arm in her grandmother's and went down the steps to the path worn between the two cottages.

"I think I'll fix a casserole, just in case," Inez mused more to herself than to Paloma.

"It's such a beautiful day. I think I'll ask Pop if he'd like to take a walk. Want to come with us?"

Inez shook her head. "You know me. I'm a house person. One walk is more than enough for me. You go and have a nice time. I'll start getting things ready for lunch."

❦

"Smell that clean air," Paloma said as she pushed Mex's wheelchair along the path covered with dry, brittle leaves and pine needles left over from the previous fall.

"I thought at one time to retire here. That was your grandmother's dream and mine...well, more mine than hers." His voice was edged with accepted sadness. But I think we will go to Mexico for our declining years. The cold is getting to me more each year."

Paloma kissed the top of his head. "Don't talk about declining years. You're getting stronger each day. And if you want to retire to Mexico where your family is, then I think it's a good idea."

"Do you? Do you really?" He glanced up at her, surprise flashing through his eyes.

She nodded. "Raul and I were thinking the same thing. Maybe have a place here in the summer and a place there in the winter and maybe a place in Little Havana near his folks so we can visit both families."

"That's sounds nice."

He reached back and placed his hand over hers. "I'm getting into the winter of my life and I start thinking. Sometimes the thoughts aren't too pleasant."

Paloma swallowed hard. It was terrible watching someone you love growing older and feeling their years. This sounded like depression, which was just as bad as the stroke. Damn the stroke! It had taken years off his life. What was he now anyway? Sixty-four? No, sixty-five last

April. She was determined to make the rest of his life as happy as possible.

"Why did you stay here instead of going back to Mexico after you made your money?"

"For my family. I wanted them to have whatever I could spare. After my father died, my mother had only my two sisters to look after her. I wanted to make sure her life was as good as I could make it."

"What about your brothers?"

He nodded. "They were in Mexico too. Wages were and are thin at best. They had their own families to look after. No, taking care of my mother was left to me."

"I know. But couldn't you have helped more if you had returned home?"

"No. Their lives wouldn't have been as good if I had returned. Besides, I had you to think about. You had grown up here. I couldn't just yank you away from your friends. But now that you have a family of your own, I'm thinking a lot about returning to my homeland and what family I have left."

Visions of the small, robust woman with white hair knotted atop her head flashed through Paloma's mind. "How old is Grandmama Rosetta now?"

"The same as the year. She was born in 1900 so she is the same as the current year."

"I've always loved to visit her. I'd like the kids to meet her."

Mex laughed and nodded. "They will. *Si*, I think she will outlive us all."

Paloma set the brake on the wheelchair and parked it at the lake's edge. She sat on a large rock nearby.

Mex reached down and picked up several flat pebbles and skipped them across the smooth water.

His laugh rang out and his eyes sparkled as he glanced at her. "See, the old man isn't too old yet. I can still skip a stone."

"Let me try." Paloma retrieved a flat, smooth stone from the shore and flicked her wrist over the water as he had taught her years ago. "Ha! I haven't lost it either."

"You know, Paloma, the doctor says with a little more therapy, I should be walking with a cane."

Paloma's face lit up. "That's wonderful. So, you'll be taking the business away from me?" she teased.

Mex shook his head. "No. But I think you should take it away from yourself."

Paloma kneeled before him, a frown replacing the teasing expression. "What do you mean?"

"I mean you have a good husband. He is a good provider and you should sell Espenoza Plumbing and Heating and help your husband in his business. After all, he travels around."

Paloma rose swiftly to her feet. "I never thought of selling the business."

"I know you haven't. But if Inez and I move to Mexico, then you aren't committed to stay here. If you want to travel with Raul, you can."

"Pop, are you sure? Really sure?"

He nodded. "I've never been more sure of anything in my life."

"But you built the business up from scratch."

"I know. And it has done all I dreamed and more. Now is the time to retire it to someone else."

"I'll have to think about this."

He skipped another stone. "I thought you would. But I know you will come to the right conclusion."

"Which is to sell and follow my husband?"

The gulls circled overhead and gave loud cries as they dove into the water, thinking the stones they flipped were meals for them.

Paloma sat down on her rock again, her knees pulled under her chin. "I think maybe you're right."

"I was hoping you'd say that."

She playfully punched him in the shoulder. "I haven't agreed yet. I have to discuss this with Raul. We haven't talked about his permanent plans yet...I mean, we haven't made any decisions yet."

Inez met them as they rolled up the plank to the deck. She looked worried and kept wiping her hands on the plaid dish towel.

"You're back." She glanced at her husband and then at Paloma.

Mex nodded. "I told her, sort of."

"Told me?" Paloma glanced from her grandmother and then back at her grandfather.

Relief flashed through Inez's eyes. "I hope you weren't too upset, *nina*. This is something that we have thought about since your grandfather's stroke."

"Upset? About what? I don't understand."

"About our moving back to Mexico before the next winter sets in."

"This year?" Paloma gasped. "You're planning to move this year?"

"*Si*." Inez threw a questioning glance at her husband. "I thought you told her."

"Well, I did, sort of."

"*Madre Santo!*" Inez rolled her eyes. "Just like a man to botch the job." She placed her hand on Paloma's shoulder. "We've already spoken to a real-estate person about putting the house on the market."

For a moment Paloma felt as if someone had pulled the rug out from beneath her. Her heart pounded in her chest and there was a roaring in her ears. "Sell the house?" That beautiful old Victorian had been her home since she could remember. She had never thought about her grandparents ever getting rid of it.

Her grandmother slipped her arm around her. "We've handled this whole thing very badly." She glanced at her husband who mirrored her own misgivings. "If you want to keep the house, we will deed it over to you."

Paloma placed her left hand on her hip and rubbed her forehead with her other hand. Then she held up both hands as if to stop all conscious thought. "This is silly. I'm a married woman and I'm carrying on like an abandoned child." She laughed shakily.

"It isn't as if you won't be coming to visit us," her grandfather spoke up. "You just told me how you and Raul had discussed the possibility of traveling to Mexico, maybe even having a place of your own there."

"I know." Paloma began to gather her thoughts. "I just never thought about you leaving. Not really, but it is the best thing, I know that."

Her grandmother gathered her into her comforting arms. "Oh, *nina*. It is for the best. The winters are so harsh and cold. How I long for the warm land of my youth. And I would like to spend my remaining years near what family I have left."

Guilt suffused Paloma. "I am sorry. I know this is for the best. And I will speak to Raul about helping the two of you move back. Perhaps we will even stay a while ourselves this winter." She gathered them both close, slipping her arms around them, hoping they didn't see the tears that burned in her eyes.

"Hey, what's all the hugging about?" Raul sauntered up to the deck, holding a string of nice-sized sunfish.

"Pop and Gram are moving back to Mexico to retire."

"Really?" Raul put the fish down on the deck. "This sounds very much like the plans Paloma and I have been tossing around."

"Yes. She has been telling us." Mex wheeled backward.

"Careful." Inez grabbed his chair. "We don't want to fish you out of the water *viejo hombre*."

Mex shot her a disgruntled look. "Old man? You called me an old man?" He turned to Paloma and Raul. "Did you hear what she called me? Old man indeed!"

Inez slipped her arms around him and tenderly rested her chin atop his head. "You will always be a young man to me. I was only teasing."

"I should hope so." Mex threw Paloma a wink as Inez wheeled him toward the cabin.

"Hey." Raul held up the string of fish. "Aren't you going to clean these after the kids and I went to all the work of catching them for you?"

Inez fought the smile that creased the corners of her mouth. "Don't go soft-soaping me, young man. You're going to clean those fish yourself. I will cook them but I refuse to clean them."

"All right. I'll clean 'em." He winked. "But I think we should celebrate tonight and have the fish tomorrow. What do you say?"

"Celebrate?" Rick raced to the deck with Gabby close behind. "What are we celebrating?"

"This fantastic vacation, our new family, anything you want. It's a day for celebration." Raul ruffled his son's hair.

Gabby lifted her hand and proudly displayed the biggest fish of them all. "Look what I caught." She held it out for all to see."

"Quit bragging," Rick grumbled.

"This is something else to celebrate." Raul placed his arm around Gabby. "Not every first-time fisherman gets the biggest catch of the day. I say that's cause for celebration."

"Take the fishing equipment back to the cottage and we'll put the fish on ice until tomorrow." Raul handed Rick his rod.

"That's settled then." Paloma linked her arm through Raul's. "What time do you want to go?"

Both Mex and Inez shrugged and glanced at each other. "Anytime is fine with us," Mex said.

"We'll pick you up at seven. How's that?" Raul asked.

"Anything you say. You're driving," Mex replied. "But I think I'll have myself a little nap before we go."

Everything was working out better than planned. Life was turning around and all their troubles seemed far behind them. Paloma felt happy and content, really happy for the first time in a long time.

"I have just one more suggestion," Mex broke in on her wanderings. "I know this nice place in Manistique that serves the best ribs you've ever tasted."

Raul shrugged at Paloma and she looked quizzical. "It doesn't make any difference to us," Paloma replied. "Just as long as the food is good."

❦

The celebration dinner was everything Paloma had expected. The small but elegant restaurant had delicious food. Mex had his ribs and everyone else, including the kids, had exactly what they wanted. The gathering was just what a family celebration should be.

Paloma rested against the seat of her grandfather's Explorer. Rick and Gabby were giggling in the luggage area as if making some sort of mischievous plans. Her grandparents were quiet, as was Raul who sat behind the wheel, maneuvering the vehicle down the now dark, single lane road cut through dense growth.

When the Explorer rounded the last bend, its lights hit a small, red sports car parked in front of Mex's cabin.

"Who could that be, this time of night?" Paloma righted herself.

"I don't know of anyone who would come out here this late at night." Mex leaned forward looking at the car.

Raul parked beside the little car.

"Oh, no," he groaned as the dark-haired woman unfolded herself from the car.

"It's about time you got back," Helena said. "I've been waiting for over three hours."

"You didn't have to on my account." Raul got out, anger deeply etched on his face. "What do you want?"

Helen smiled and moved confidently toward him. "I've come to collect Rick, of course. His vacation is over." She motioned toward the car. "Come on, Rick. Get your things. We're leaving."

Raul stepped between her and the boy. "Over my dead body. I told you when you phoned you'd never get him back again."

The woman purred. "Don't be silly. You knew this was just an itsy-bitsy vacation. It's time for Rick to come home."

Rick stepped to Raul. "Dad, do I have to? Do I have to go back?" His voice quivered.

"No son, you don't. I'll take care of this."

The woman's face turned angry. "Now look here. I have custody and..."

She didn't get any more words out before another car gunned down the dusty land and came to a screeching halt in front of them.

"I'm late again." Gomez emerged from his little yellow Volkswagen Rabbit. "I thought for sure I'd beat her here."

"Who the hell are you?" Helena shouted.

"I got everything you'll need to keep her from having custody of your son." Gomez held out his little black book and motioned toward Helena.

Raul looked at Paloma. "Take everyone into the cabin. I'll be there shortly." His voice was full of contempt, sparked with anger, but not with Paloma. Never with Paloma.

"Now, see here—" Helena began again, but Raul cut her off.

"No, you see here." Raul grabbed her by the arm and led her to her car. "You've caused enough trouble to last the rest of my life. Now get your greedy body out of here before I do something we'll both be sorry for."

She yanked open the car door but she wasn't through yet. "That boy is mine. You have no right to him."

"He's my son," Raul said in deadly earnest.

She laughed. "Your son. Yours and who else's? I told you he was not your natural son. I am blood to him. The courts have already given him to me."

Raul fought to control the consuming anger raging through his body. "Helena, you get away from here and don't you ever try to see Rick again."

"In your dreams. I'll have you in jail for this."

"I don't think so. Gomez here has been on your tail long enough to get some pretty good information the judge would be interested in seeing."

Helena frowned at Gomez. "Who?"

"Private investigator, Gomez Vega." Gomez gave an exaggerated bow from the waist.

"Private inv..." She suddenly seemed speechless, as if for the first time it sunk in she didn't have the upper hand.

Gomez stepped forward, still waving the book. "And some pretty interesting information I have too."

She swallowed hard and glared at Raul. "You had me investigated?"

He shrugged. "You forced me to."

"You may have bought yourself a little time, but I'll still regain custody of Rick, you wait and see."

Raul shook his head. "I don't think so. Not this time. Not when the judge sees what you've been up to. Not when he knows his father wants him."

She crossed her arms over her breasts. "And just what has your friend got?" She glared at him.

"If Gomez says he has something on you, he has something."

"You don't even know," she said with a sneer.

"Does last Friday night mean anything to you?" Gomez cut in.

A dead silence stood between them. Helena glanced from one to the other.

"Like I said. If Gomez says he has something on you, he's got something."

"But, you're not his father."

"So you've told me a hundred times. But this time I think we'll let the paternity tests do the talking. I've been watching Rick. He looks exactly as I did at that age. I think a paternity test will surprise you if you really believe that."

Now this did stop her and she stood before them dumbfounded.

Raul arched a brow. "What? Nothing to say? Perhaps you've known all along I was Rick's father."

Helena bit her lower lip. "You're crazy. I ought to know who the father of my child was and it certainly isn't you."

"As I said, we'll let the tests prove it. Now I suggest you get out of here. If you want to see me again, it will be in court with my lawyer."

"You haven't seen the last of me." She threw herself into her car and yanked the door shut with such a bang it rattled the window. The motor jumped to life and the tires threw dirt and gravel when she spun down the road.

"Whoa." Gomez stared after her. "That's a nasty piece of work if I've ever seen one."

There was only one thing left to do. A paternity test needed to be taken as soon as they got back. Helena was nasty, just as Gomez said. He had to have the proof that Rick was his. And if he wasn't? Well, that didn't matter. He'd never give him up. Rick was his son, blood or not.

"Raul?" Paloma slowly crept down the porch. "Is everything all right?"

His face was taut and strained. He gathered her into his arms and rested his face in her hair. "We're going to have to fight her in court. But let's not let the kids know."

"What about tomorrow? And Fayette?"

Raul tightened his hold. "We're still going. Helena won't stop us from showing the kids a good time."

Chapter Twelve

After assuring her grandparents everything was all right and saying goodnight, everyone went back to the new cabin where Paloma put on a pot of fresh coffee. Raul assured Rick everything was going to be all right and sent both children to bed.

Paloma set out the sugar and cream. "Helena has a way of destroying a great evening."

"She won't be causing you much more trouble. I've got enough information on that little gal. No judge in his right mind would give her custody of Rick."

"I hope so. I know Raul is worried even though he hides it well."

Raul strode across the room. "I just checked the kids and they're out like a light." She handed Gomez a steaming cup.

"I'm surprised." Raul sipped the hot brew. "I thought for sure the upset with Helena would cause Rick a sleepless night."

Paloma smiled and sat down at the wooden table, her right leg tucked beneath her. "It's this fresh northern air. It tires kids out. Besides, kids take things better than we expect them to. He didn't have to go with her, so as far as he's concerned, everything's all right."

Raul was silent for several seconds. "So? What are we going to do?"

Gomez shrugged matter-of-factly. "I don't think there's going to be a problem. But the first thing is to get that paternity test, then file with the court for parental custody."

Raul's face darkened. "All right. Then what if he isn't my son?"

Paloma reached out and placed a reassuring hand on Raul's arm. "He's your son. All you have to do is look at him. He's the spitting image of you."

"I think so too, but what if by some outside chance he isn't?" His eyes appealed to Gomez.

Gomez shook his head complacently. "Look, I told you I have enough evidence of her unfitness as a mother. You don't have any worries. If by some outside chance you aren't Rick's natural father, you're still the only father he's ever known. Helena will never get custody of him again. You have my word." He took a drink of the coffee Paloma poured for him. "And I read your ex's body language tonight. When you threatened her with the paternity test and court, that threw her a loop. She isn't so sure anymore. Besides we have my little black book." He held it up and waved it like a sword.

"You think?" Raul seemed relieved.

"I know," Gomez answered. "That little lady was struck dumb for a few seconds. And from what I've observed of her, it takes a lot to unnerve her. She's one hard cookie."

Raul heaved a sigh of relief. "I hope you're right."

⁂

They did take the kids to Fayette and stayed at Mackinac Island overnight, just as planned. A slight storm cloud hung over them for the rest of the vacation.

⁂

"Home at last. Petoskey has never looked so good." Raul pulled into the Espenoza drive so Paloma could pick up a few things she needed.

"A vacation is always welcome, but coming home feels good too," Paloma agreed.

"How long did Mex say they were staying at the cabin?"

"Gram said about another three weeks. Pop told me to go ahead and show the house to the real estate people if they called."

"Are you sure you want to have them sell? I saw your face when Mex mentioned selling."

Paloma stepped from the truck and glanced around at the old Victorian that had been her home most of her life. "I've always loved this house."

"Then why sell?"

Paloma turned to Raul. "What do you mean? It's their house. If they want to sell they can. I wouldn't ask them not to."

He slipped his arm around her. "I know, but we could buy it. It would still be your home for as long as you want."

The heavy lashes that shadowed her cheeks flew up in surprise. "Buy it? You'd do that?"

He laughed and pulled her close. "Of course. This could be our summer home if you like, or our permanent home, whatever you wish."

She gently pulled away, cocked her head and smiled broadly. "You surprise me, Mr. Fernandez."

"Why? Because I want to please my wife and make her happy?"

She leaned forward, rose on her toes and kissed him.

"Oh, yuk!" Rick groused when he and Gabby came from the other side of the truck. "Will you guys quit that!"

Raul lifted his head. "Sorry, sport. I'm afraid you'll be seeing a lot of this." He pulled Paloma close. They both laughed, happiness spilling into the quiet May day.

Raul began taking the large cases and coolers from the back. "Rick. Take these and put them back where you found them." He tossed him the camping gear they'd borrowed from Mex.

"Are you and Dad really going to buy this house?" Rick asked Paloma.

"I think so." She threw a meaningful glance Raul's way.

Raul threw his son the last duffle bag. "Would you like that, son?"

"I don't know. That logger is a man's house." Rick's face shadowed.

"That place is just a rental. This would be our house." Raul threw his own fishing gear into the back of his truck.

"Catch." Gabby playfully threw one of the duffle bags at Rick.

"Hey, watch that," he warned.

Paloma watched the easy exchange between her daughter and Rick. She was coming around, getting involved with things. Rick helped Raul put things back in the back of the pickup and Gabby walked toward Paloma. "What would you say if Raul and I bought this house?"

"It's a great house as long as I can keep the bedroom I had the first night."

Paloma laughed. "I'm sure that can be arranged with no problem."

"Rick and I got something to show you." Gabby took a long sketch pad from atop one of the coolers.

"What?"

"Rick and I are going to draw a cartoon comic book together. He's a great artist. You ought to see his sketches." She held out the book to Paloma.

"Yeah and you oughta see hers." Rick rushed up and took the pad from Paloma's hand. He flipped through the pages. "Look at this."

On the page was a sketch of a cartoon character that looked as if it had come out of a Marvel comic book.

"You did this?" Paloma turned to Raul. "Did you see this?"

He glanced over Paloma's shoulder and whistled. "That is good."

Gabby colored. "It's okay," she whispered.

"Okay? It's better than okay. You are an artist, my girl."

"Rick is just as good." She turned several pages to show them.

Paloma and Raul glanced at Rick.

"Looks like we have some real talent in the family," Raul laughed. "Are you and these two artists ready to go?"

Paloma glanced up at Raul. "I have some things I want to pack up and take to the log house. I'll be a little while. Why don't you and Rick go unpack and Gabby can help me?"

"All right. Rick and I can put our things away and then come pick you gals up for a bite to eat, how'd that be?"

"Sounds good to me." Paloma reached for one of Raul's duffle bags that had yet to be reloaded and threw it at him. The action was so quick, she took him off guard.

"Go, girl." Gabby joined in the fun and tossed her bag at Raul, followed by Rick.

Raul held up his hands. "Hey, I give up. You can't all gang up on me at once here."

"The heck we can't!" Rick tackled him around the legs and both tumbled to the ground. Gabby jumped in, laughing so hard she had tears in her eyes.

"I said, I give up," Raul yelled playfully, rolling away from two pairs of tickling fingers. "Give an old man a break."

"All right, kids. Enough is enough." Paloma came to the rescue. "If I want to get my packing done, we best get at it." She reached over and tweaked Gabby's nose.

"Oh, all right." Gabby rose and brushed the driveway dust from her jeans.

"Come on, champ. Let's go home and unpack."

"Aw, gee. Can't I stay here? There's not much to unpack. I can do it later."

Raul threw an appealing look in Paloma's direction, but she just cocked her head and shrugged.

"A lot of help you are," he complained.

"Let him stay. You can come back after you unload the truck."

"Sounds great to me." Rick beamed. "Where we gonna eat?"

"I don't know. How about a steak at Shelde's?" Raul said.

"All right. Let's synchronize our watches. It's four-thirty, so be sure to be here at six."

"Six it is." He bent and kissed her full on the lips.

"Ugh, there you go again."

Raul turned and ruffled Rick's hair. "You just wait. Your day's coming, pal. I can give as good as I get."

"Okay, okay, I was just teasing." Rick raced toward the house as Raul climbed into the truck and pulled away.

Paloma had just got to the door, when a truck screeched into the drive. Raul. What had he forgotten, she wondered, turning around. Nothing that she could see.

"Paloma!" Carl's voice echoed through the afternoon air. "Paloma, I want a word with you."

A knot twisted from the pit of her stomach right up to her neck, choking off her breath.

"Carl. What a surprise."

He didn't wait to be invited in, he burst in, anger written across his face. "You think you're pretty smart, don't you?"

Paloma stepped back. "I don't know what you mean."

"The hell you don't." He raked his fingers through his blond hair. "You made a fool of me. A laughing stock with the men. We had an understanding, you and me. We were engaged and you go off with that bastard Raul. He's the father of your daughter, isn't he?" He barely stopped to catch his breath when he raced on. "I hear you found her in Kalamazoo. Are you one happy family now?"

Paloma was shocked anew at such violent anger in one she had once prepared to build a life with. "Carl, this isn't doing anyone any good."

"What the hell do you know about how I feel? I wouldn't have you back on a bet, but I wanted you to know what I think of you and Raul."

"Is it true?"

For the first time Paloma saw Gabby standing at the top of the stairs, gripping the railing with knuckles as white as her face.

"Gabby."

"Is it? Is he right? Are you my real mother?" Her dark eyes were as big as saucers as she slowly came down the stairs.

"So this is the daughter!" Carl glared at the girl coming slowly down the stairs.

"Get out!" Paloma got her bearings and yanked open the door, her anger crushing down any fear she had at first felt.

"You don't have to ask twice. I'm leaving."

Her face felt hot and her heart was beating so fast she thought it would burst. "And you're fired."

He turned, a sneer spreading across his face. "You can't fire me, I quit."

"Good!" She slammed the door so hard she was surprised the glass didn't shatter into a million pieces.

"Paloma?" Gabby stood on the first landing. "Are you my mother?"

"Gabby, we have to talk."

"No!" Gabby screamed, tears washing down her face. "Answer me. Are you?"

Paloma nodded. "Yes, but you must let me explain. I didn't want to give you up, but I had to." She reached out to her in appeal, but Gabby backed away. "I wanted you to have two parents that loved you, not just a mother who couldn't give you the family you needed." She gasped for air. Gabby had to understand. She had to know she loved her, that she hadn't wanted to give her up.

"I couldn't take care of you. I..."

"I don't care!" Gabby cried and covered her ears. "You gave me away like a broken toy. You didn't want me either." Her voice broke on a sob.

"Gabby, that's not true. I wanted to keep you. That's why I came to find you and when I did, you had run away. I had to find you. I love you. I've always loved you." Her sobs matched her daughter's, her outstretched hand trembled.

Gabby shook her head and inched her way down the rest of the stairs. "I don't believe you. You're a liar!" she screamed. "I hate you!" She yanked the door open and ran out.

"I'll go find her." Rick raced down the stairs.

Paloma watched dumbfounded as both children raced down the sidewalk and disappeared around the cedar hedge.

Oh, God, what now? Fear gripped her. Damn Carl for causing this catastrophe!

"Raul," she whispered. Grabbing the phone she dialed his number, moving up and down on her toes while she waited anxiously for him to answer.

"Come on, answer."

"Hello?"

"Oh, God, Raul." Her voice cracked and one sob after another ripped from her lips.

"Paloma? What's wrong?"

"Raul...Carl...Gabby..."

"Paloma! Calm down and tell me what's wrong." Raul forced himself to keep his voice calm and reassuring.

"Carl told Gabby I'm her mother. She's run away again. Rick's gone after her."

"What?"

"She knows. Gabby knows and she hates me. She said she hates me," Paloma sobbed.

"Stay right there. I'll be there in five minutes. They can't have gotten far." There was a definite click cutting the phone dead.

Paloma paced back and forth in the foyer, watching the clock as the hands refused to move. Five minutes he had said. The clock hands weren't moving. She stepped toward it. Stop it. He'll be here. He said he would and he will. Get a grip. This is no time to fall to pieces.

A screech of tires announced Raul's arrival.

Paloma pulled open the door and rushed into Raul's arms. "We've got to find them." She raced toward the truck and looked back when Raul didn't follow. She frowned. "Aren't you coming?"

"We have to wait here. I called Gomez and then the police. They both said to wait right here and they will come in a few minutes."

Panic squeezed the breath from Paloma's lungs. "We can't just stand here. They're out there somewhere. We've got to find them."

"We're not going to help anyone by not doing as the authorities say." He gripped her shoulders.

"I have to find her." She tried to twist away, but he held tight.

"You can't. The police will know better how to find them. Just calm down and wait until they get here."

"No!" She twisted hysterically to get free. "I have to find her. It's my fault. All my fault." She gave way tears. "Everything's my fault."

He cradled her in his arms. "It's no one's fault, except perhaps Carl's. We'll find her...together. And we'll make her understand what happened."

Before Paloma could respond, a police car swung into the drive followed by Gomez's little yellow bug.

"What happened?" Gomez strode in front of the police officer.

Raul with his arm still around Paloma told Gomez everything that had happened after their return.

"They can't have gotten far. We'll find 'em."

Paloma leaned her head against Raul's chest. "They're just babies. Anything could happen to them." Soft sobs escaped her quivering lips.

Gomez reached out and placed a comforting hand on her arm. "Gabby is street-wise. She'll be all right. This is northern Michigan, not Detroit. Unless they go into hiding, they won't be hard to find."

"Really?" Paloma's heart grasped at the hope Gomez was offering.

"That's right. There's a lot of open land up here. They'll be spotted."

The police officer who had been talking to one of the neighbors across the street came back holding his little black pad in his hands. "Your neighbor, Mrs. Conway, said she saw two kids getting into a little red sports car."

"Helena!" Raul snapped.

Oh, God, no! Helena was dangerous and angry. She would do anything to get at Raul's money. "Raul?" She glanced at him, her eyes flashing the terror she felt. "Where's he going?" Paloma reached out toward the departing police officer. "What's he doing? He can't leave."

"It's all right. He's going to radio in what we know and suspect. He'll give a description of Helena, the kids and her car. There'll be an all-points bulletin. If Helena has the kids, she won't get away."

The officer got out of his car and stepped toward them. "I called in the information. She can't get far. We'll have her picked up shortly."

Paloma gripped Raul's arm. "What if they don't? What if she takes the kids away."

Raul pulled her close. "She won't. The police know what they're doing."

Oh, why had she taken the easy way out and given Gabby up for adoption? What was she thinking? It had devastated her to give that child away. If she'd kept her, none of this would ever have happened, so it was her fault.

"Let's go inside and wait. That's all we can do now." Raul led a reluctant Paloma toward the house.

"I'd like a cup of coffee before I set out. You never know when I'll bet back in. Do you have any?" Gomez asked.

"I'll make some. It won't take a minute." Paloma moved into the house, leaving the two men standing on the sidewalk.

With a backward glance she observed their heads together, a serious conversation transpiring. Had they conspired to get her out of the way so they could talk? If so, what were they talking about that she couldn't hear? Did Gomez know something he thought would upset her?

"Where is Gomez?" Paloma asked when Raul came inside without him.

His eyes settled on the coffee pot dripping fresh coffee. "Oh, he couldn't wait. He had to get going."

"Raul, don't lie to me! What's going on?"

He frowned and shook his head. "I don't know what you mean."

"Yes, you do. Gomez wanted to get me in the house so he could talk to you alone. That's why he asked me to make some coffee."

"No, he was in a hurry, that's all."

"Stop it!" Paloma cried, clasping her hands to her chest. "Don't you dare stand there and lie to me. Gabby is my child. I have every right to know what's wrong."

Raul's face paled slightly as he drew in a deep breath. "Gomez is just concerned about the worst and didn't want you to hear him suggest that anything could go wrong."

The color drained from her face. "What does he suspect?" She reached for a kitchen chair to steady herself.

Raul poured himself a cup of hot coffee. "He's a little concerned about Helena. He's worried what she'll do. Especially since her sugar daddy has abandoned her."

Paloma raced to the door and grabbed her coat from the peg on the wall. "Come on. We're going to look for the kids. I don't care if we have to look under every rock in northern Michigan, we're going to find our kids."

His breath came fast and harsh as he reached out and grabbed her. "And just where are you going to look that the police haven't already thought of?"

"I don't know." In a fury of fear and impatience she twisted to free herself. "But I can't just stay here. I have to look." She fought his hold.

"Don't be an idiot. We have to stay here. What if the kids call and no one answers?"

She quieted a few moments to catch her breath and think about what he'd just said. It was true. If they tried to call and no one answered...

Almost immediately it started to rain. Paloma looked out the kitchen window as the rain came down in sheets, pelting the window with such force it sounded like hail.

The children were out in this. If they didn't get shelter, they could get pneumonia. But then, they weren't out in it. They were with Helena, God knows where.

She sat on the chair, her head in her hands and sobbed. "It's all my fault. If I hadn't given her up, none of this would have happened."

Raul pulled her into the circle of his arms. "I've told you before. It's no one's fault. And we'll find them, I promise."

Before Paloma could respond, both the doorbell and telephone rang. They glanced at each other.

"You get the door, I'll answer the phone," Raul said.

Paloma raced through the dining room to the hall and threw the door open. Her heart was beating rapidly. "Thank God!" she exclaimed when she saw Gomez with a very wet Rick and Gabby.

Without thinking, she embraced both kids.

"They're a little wet, but no worse for the wear." Gomez came in as soaked as the kids. "I found them hitch hiking down 131."

"That was the police." Raul's voice echoed as he moved into the dining room. "They found Helena, but no kids..." He stopped dead when he saw Gomez and the kids.

He turned away for a few seconds. When he turned back he shook his index finger at them both. "I'm so glad and angry at the same time, I don't know whether to hug or spank you. Do you know what you've put us through?"

"I couldn't let her go alone," Rick explained. "She'd get into trouble and then I'd never forgive myself for not helping her."

"I know. I know." Raul nodded. "Both of you go upstairs and get into dry clothes."

Rick's expression darkened. "I don't have any clean clothes here. What am I supposed to wear?"

"Draw a bath in the main bathroom. We'll think of something later," Paloma said as she turned to Gabby who stood with her gaze glued to the floor.

"And you, young lady. Take a bath and get into some warm, dry clothes. We'll talk later." Paloma's voice was not sharp, but it wasn't soft and gentle either.

Raul and Paloma stood looking at each other until Paloma finally broke the silence.

"Why don't you take Gomez in the kitchen and get him that cup of coffee he wanted so badly earlier." She threw Gomez a mocking look.

"Hey, why not?" Gomez slapped Raul on the shoulder. "Come on. I think Paloma wants to be alone with the kids."

Paloma moved slowly up the stairs, her legs like lead weights. She went into her bedroom and took the box down from her closet shelf. Holding it in her ice cold hands, she stepped into Gabby's room. Sounds of water splashing echoed from the closed bathroom door.

"Gabby. If you're finished, I'd like to talk to you."

"Go away. I don't want to talk to you," Gabby answered.

Paloma rolled her eyes toward the ceiling. Keep calm. This was not the time to have an argument with a distressed child. "I'm not leaving. You might just as well come out here and get this over with."

Slowly the door opened and Gabby emerged wrapped in a thick, floor-length pink terry robe. Her face was set in stone, showing no emotion. "I don't want to hear it."

Paloma glanced at the box in her hands. "Sit down. I want to show you something." She sat on the edge of Gabby's bed.

Gabby sat in the rocker, obviously not wanting to share the bed with Paloma.

"In here is all I have of you as a baby." She lifted the lid and held up the pink plastic bracelet. "I stole this from you when the nurse wasn't looking." She handed it to Gabby.

Paloma's eyes filled with tears that slipped down her face. "I even clipped a little of your hair and put it on this Scotch tape." She smiled and held up the soft, dark curl. "You had such a head of hair, not bald like a lot of babies."

"Why?"

"Why did I give you up for adoption?"

Gabby nodded.

"Because I was young, unmarried and afraid of what my grandparents would say. I didn't have a job to provide for you and I wanted you to have a family with a mother and a father." She shrugged and wiped the tears from her face. "I got you half the deal. You had a mother who loved you dearly."

"Yes, she did," Gabby whispered softly.

Paloma nodded. "That's what I wanted for you, but I wanted you to have a father too. I'm sorry that part of the deal didn't work out."

"Did you ever think of me?" Bitterness rested around Gabby's words.

Paloma gulped back a sob as she reached out and took Gabby's hand in her own. "I carried you in my body for nine months, but I carried you in my heart for eleven years."

More tears fell unchecked. "Wait right here." Paloma rose and raced into her room and returned with a larger box in her hands. "I haven't looked at these for years. I just add one more on your birthday."

"What are they?"

"Birthday cards."

"Mine?"

Paloma nodded. "I got you one each year and tied it in with all the others. I even wrote little notes to you, even though I never thought you'd get a chance to read them."

"May I have them?"

"Of course." Paloma handed her the stack of envelopes tied in a pink ribbon.

Tears glistened in Gabby's eyes as she held the envelopes and the pink identification bracelet in her hands.

Before either could say another word, a knock announced Raul as he opened the door. "Is this a private party, or can anyone come in?"

Paloma raised a questioning eyebrow, leaving the answer in Gabby's court.

"And you're my father, right?"

"Yes, I am." He sat on the edge of the bed beside Paloma. "I know how hard this is for you."

Gabby's expression went grim. "How can you know?"

"Because I didn't learn until a few weeks ago that I was your father. But I am your father and we're a family, you, Paloma, Rick and me. And I'll go through hell and high-water to stay a family."

Gabby wiped the tears away with the back of her hand. "I don't know." More tears fell. "I'm so confused."

Paloma slipped from the bed and knelt beside her daughter. "This has all happened so fast, so harshly. But your father and I love you. We want to build a family unit you can be proud of. All we ask is, give us a try. Haven't we had a lot of good times already?"

Gabby sniffed and nodded.

"There'll be a lot more, I promise."

Raul dropped to his knee before his daughter. "And I add my promise to your mother's. Please, give us a chance to prove how much we love and want you."

"Does that include me?" Rick stood in the doorway.

Raul held out his hand to his son. "Of course it does. Come tell your sister how much you want her to be part of our family."

Rick moved into the room, his hands stuffed deep in his pockets. "Aw, heck. She already knows that. I told her when she ran away she was doing the wrong thing, but she wouldn't listen to me." He stepped back into the hall.

"Come in, son." Raul motioned him inside.

"I...I don't belong here."

"What's wrong?" Raul asked.

"I'm not really part of the family, am I? I heard Mom telling you I wasn't really your son."

Raul rose and crossed the room to his son. "You are my son and have been since the minute you were born." He took the boy in his arms.

Rick pulled back. "But not really your son. Not your flesh and blood son."

"Does it really matter?"

"Yeah, it does."

Paloma's heart was breaking for the both of them. She moved across the room and turned each of them to the full-length mirror beside the door. "Just look at that and tell me you don't believe you are really father and son."

"What do you mean?" Rick asked.

"You are the spitting image of your father. If you aren't his son, then no one is."

Raul turned to Rick. "But if it will make you feel any better we'll have a paternity test taken. That will prove you are my son."

"Then Mom won't try to take me away ever again?"

"Never again." Raul pulled Rick close.

Paloma turned her attention to Gabby. "Well? Are you going to make it unanimous?"

Gabby stared at each one of them and then at her letters. "I have a brother. A real blood brother?" Her eyes settled on Rick.

"Yes, Rick is your brother," Paloma assured her.

"Then I guess I want to be part of the family." She raced across the room and threw herself in the middle of the trio.

Raul was the first to speak after that total display of family devotion. "I think we better go down and tell Gomez the good news. He's leaving, you know."

"Where? Where's he going?" Paloma asked.

"He's been offered a job in California and will be leaving in the morning."

Together as a united family they went down to say goodbye to Gomez. And to begin building a family circle strong enough to handle any trouble that might come their way. Paloma knew there would be hard times ahead, times that would try the soul, but they were a family now and together they would overcome all obstacles. She had Raul's love, he had hers and together that love would be the tie that binds.